A MOMENT IN CRIME

ALSO AVAILABLE BY AMANDA ALLEN

Santa Fe Revival Mysteries

Sante Fe Mourning

Elizabethan Mysteries
(written as Amanda Carmack)

Murder at Fontainebleau

Murder at Whitehall

Murder in the Queen's Garden

Murder at Westminster Abbey

Murder at Hatfield House

A Moment in Crime

A SANTA FE REVIVAL MYSTERY

Amanda Allen

CROOKED
LANE

NEW YORK

Copyright © 2018 by Amanda McCabe

Published in the United States by Crooked Lane Books, an imprint of The Quick Brown Fox & Company LLC.

Crooked Lane Books and its logo are trademarks of The Quick Brown Fox & Company LLC.

Library of Congress Catalog-in-Publication data available upon request.

ISBN (hardcover): 978-1-68331-881-1
ISBN (ePub): 978-1-68331-882-8
ISBN (ePDF): 978-1-68331-883-5

Cover design by Lori Palmer
Book design by Jennifer Canzone

Printed in the United States.

www.crookedlanebooks.com

Crooked Lane Books
34 West 27th St., 10th Floor
New York, NY 10001

First Edition: December 2018

10 9 8 7 6 5 4 3 2 1

PROLOGUE

New York City, 1910

"What are you going to be, Maddie? When you're a grown-up lady, I mean," Gwendolyn asked, suddenly breaking the dusty silence of their attic sanctuary.

Maddie glanced up from her sketchbook, startled. She'd become so absorbed in her drawing, the scene of a summer meadow with a castle in the background, that she had completely forgotten where she really was. That she wasn't alone.

Not that she minded being with Gwen at all. In fact, her cousin was very nearly her favorite person in the world, certainly in her family. Gwen's father was one of Maddie's mother's Astor cousins, and when they visited the Vaughns' Fifth Avenue house there were games, bicycle rides, trips to Central Park, and long, lavish teas where the grown-ups droned on with their boring gossip for hours, but Maddie, Gwen, and their brothers were left to make their own fun.

Best of all were the times when Maddie and Gwen could slip off by themselves and sneak up to the attic storage room tucked behind the maids' chambers at the very top of the tall house made to look like a château. There, among the trunks and piles of old furniture, they would read and chatter and draw, and fritter away the time in dusty sunlight from the high windows. No mothers or nannies hovered to tell them to stand up straight or comb their hair or quit running, to act like proper ladies.

Being a proper lady was hideously boring.

"I don't know," Maddie answered honestly, trying to consider Gwen's question. "We're only thirteen."

In truth, she wasn't sure she *wanted* to know the answer. Grown-up ladyhood seemed to be a world full of rules that were no fun at all. The hats seemed nice; she would give ladyhood that much. The enormous confections of feathers and flowers her mother perched on her upswept pile of dark hair were pretty. But everything else looked dreary in the extreme. Walking slowly, smiling calmly, never talking too much, never showing too much interest in anything but babies and gossip. She couldn't look forward to it.

Maddie glanced down at her drawing. *That* was what she liked more than anything. Art, making new worlds with just a pencil or paintbrush. When she was painting, nothing else mattered at all. Everything disappeared, and she saw only what was on her paper. Her mother's disappointed frowns, her father's vague smiles on the rare times he was home, her brother's annoying pranks—none of it was there.

She thought of the artists she saw with their easels in the park or along the marble halls of the Metropolitan Museum. The colors and lines that brought so many things to vivid life where she stood and watched, awestruck. The artists were usually men, of course, but her mother's best friend, Millicent Schuyler, owned a portrait by Berthe Morisot, and Maddie's art teacher at Miss Spence's School was always putting her work on display at galleries. Maybe, just maybe, Maddie could be a real artist herself someday. Even teaching art could be interesting.

"I suppose you'll marry Peter," Gwen said, all casual and dismissive.

Startled, because her own thoughts on the future were so different, Maddie turned to her cousin. Gwen sat in the window seat, her legs swinging, the pale sunlight turning her silvery blonde hair to a sweep of fairy-spun gold. Sometimes people were surprised the two girls were related, as Maddie was so small and dark, Gwen so blonde.

They were different in temperament, too. Gwen was vivacious, full of high jinks, and bursting with confidence, while Maddie was careful and quiet until she was sure of things. But they usually understood each other very well.

Or so Maddie had thought.

"I don't know," she answered slowly. She considered Pete Alwin, who had lived across the street forever and had always been in her life. Their mothers were in the Opera Society and the Garden League together; Pete had been her first dance partner at cotillion, and he always played with her on the summer beach at Newport. He let her sketch him often. He had such an interesting face, always smiling. His quick laugh and merry brown eyes always made any day lighter.

But she hadn't seen him in a while, not since he'd gone away to Phillip's Academy. She'd missed him, yet she'd also been wrapped up in the new extra art classes her parents permitted, the promise of a trip to Paris and possibly some classes at the École des Beaux-Arts.

"I do like Pete a lot," she said. "But I think there are some things I'd like to do before I get married."

"Like what?" Gwen popped a bonbon into her mouth, her green eyes bright with curiosity.

"Take some art classes in Paris, maybe," Maddie ventured. It was the first time she had admitted such a thing aloud as she waited for her parents to arrange the trip. If she wanted it too much, it was sure to be snatched away. "If I get to be good enough, maybe I could show a painting in a gallery."

"I think you're good enough now," Gwen said.

"Really?" Maddie gasped. No one had ever told her that before.

"Of course. Heaps better than those gloomy old flowers Mama hangs in her sitting room. Even if you did marry Peter, I doubt he'd stop you painting."

"Probably not." Maddie thought of Pete, so happy-go-lucky, so accepting of everyone around him. But then, husbands always did expect their wives to put them, their houses, and their families first. Even nice ones like Pete. It was just the way it was. "I still don't want to get married for years and years, though."

"Quite right. Even handsome boys like that Roger Godolphin, who I danced with at cotillion last month, get to be bores so quickly. All that cricket talk."

Maddie laughed as Gwen gave a shudder. "What do *you* want to be then, Gwennie?" she said, expecting her cousin would want to marry the Prince of Wales or something like that.

"I'm going to be an actress," Gwen proclaimed solemnly. "A great one. Lady Macbeth and Rosalind, all the great roles. They'll cover the stage with flowers and pull my carriage through the streets. Every girl will copy my hairstyle and wear the same hats I do."

"Really?" Maddie said, amazed at such a grand dream. But truly, if anyone could do such a thing, become an idol of the stage, it was Gwen.

Gwen frowned. "You don't think I could do it?"

"Of course you could. If anyone was ever meant to be a great, famous actress, it's you. But surely your parents would never let you!" If Maddie was lucky, her mother might let her increase her drawing classes. Art was a lady-like hobby, admired and refined, as long as it didn't go too far. But no Astor would ever be allowed to go on the public stage. Their cousin Monty had been cast out when he married an actress.

"They'll have to, won't they?" Gwen said, scowling defiantly. "They'll just have to realize this is the twenti-eth century. The world isn't like when they were young anymore. There are typewriters and motorcars, and— and airplanes! There are even bits of film in those Edison stereoscopes where we can watch people dancing. Who knows what will happen next! The world deserves to see me, don't you think?"

Maddie laughed. "They certainly do."

"And you will paint my portrait, which will make you famous, too." Gwen sat back on the window-seat cushions with a satisfied smile. "You see. Our lives are going to work out absolutely splendidly."

CHAPTER 1

Santa Fe, 1922

"When I grow up, I'm going to look just like *that*," eight-year-old Ruby Anaya sighed as she stared at a glamorous photo of Constance Talmadge in Maddie's new *Movie News* mag.

Ruby's twin, Pearl, studied the image with a gimlet eye. A blob of cookie dough from the bowl she was stirring fell right on the gleaming image of Constance's silver lamè skirt. "You'll never be blonde," she said, and tugged at her sister's glossy black plait.

Ruby pulled Pearl's hair right back. "There's peroxide, isn't there? Uncle Gunther tried some last month."

"Yes, and look what happened to poor Mr. Ryder. He has barely a curl left after he burned them off," their mother, Maddie's housekeeper, Juanita Anaya, said sternly. She barely glanced up from sewing the labels in the girls' new black-and-white school uniforms. They were starting at the Sisters of Loretto's school the next day, and there was no time to lose. "No daughter of mine will ever peroxide her hair. It's not proper."

Maddie stifled a giggle at the memory of Gunther's little hair mishap. In a misguided attempt to look more "Viking" for his new author publicity photos, he had dyed his curly red hair platinum—only to see much of it tumble out of his scalp in burned curlicues.

"Oh well, darling," he had sniffed. *"Turbans are very chic right now."*

Maddie plied her own needle on the hem of her pink chiffon dancing dress for that night's party at the Art Museum. Her own work was going to be among those on display, and she had to admit she was more than a little nervous. Not just about people seeing her paintings, but about being escorted to the soiree by the handsome Dr. David Cole. Her first real date in—well, ever, since she had married her childhood sweetheart and then lost him in the war.

"Dorothy Gish has dark hair," she said, pointing out a photo of the raven-haired comedienne in an elaborate eighteenth-century costume. "And she is very beautiful."

"More than her sister Lillian, do you think?" Juanita asked. She always tried to pretend indifference to such newfangled amusements as the movies, but Maddie knew different. It wasn't always the twins who took the piles of magazines Maddie had sent from New York out of the sitting room.

"I think they're equally lovely. Just like Ruby and Pearl," Maddie said. "I almost went to California once, you know, to see the movie sets not long after most of them went out there from New York."

The twins looked at her with wide, chocolate-brown eyes. Even Buttercup, their little terrier dog, sat up with an interested perk to her ears. "You were going to be in the movies, Señora Maddie?" Ruby gasped.

Maddie laughed. "No, not *in* the movies. Just watch some of them filming, take in the ocean and the sunshine, eat some fresh oranges right off the trees. My mother thought it would do me good."

"Do you good?" Pearl asked, her little forehead creased in concern. "Were you ill, Señora Maddie?"

Maddie carefully snipped a thread that tightened a silver bead onto pink silk, remembering that time. Wondering how much to tell the girls. Those weren't days she enjoyed thinking about at all. The weeks and months after hearing of her husband Pete's death in the trenches of France. The blackness that seemed to enclose her like a suffocating blanket, shutting out all the light, the warmth and feeling.

The girls had only just lost their father, in a terrible way. They didn't seem to be falling into the abyss as she had, since they had their mother's careful love and attention, and the excitement of a new school. Maddie kept a close watch on them, and never wanted them to worry.

But she *could* tell them about the journey, and how it had all ended for her. In a new home here in Santa Fe, in new life and hope.

"I was very tired," she said. "And I had a cousin named Gwendolyn, who always said she wanted to be an actress. She had a chance to make a screen test in California with a famous director, and she wanted me to go with her on the cross-country train trip so she wouldn't be lonely." She had also gone so Gwen wouldn't get into too much trouble, as her parents feared. They'd thought a chaperone would be good for Gwen. Aunt Astor had been right to worry, of course; Gwen had already caused numerous scandals in New York, the latest involving the fountain outside the Plaza Hotel. "My mother thought I would like the journey."

"Did you?" Ruby asked.

"Very much. I saw so many things I had only ever heard of in books. The Mississippi River, mountains and plains. But my very favorite spot was right here in Santa Fe."

"Why?" asked Pearl, who had never been further away from Santa Fe than her parents' ancestral home at San Ildefonso Pueblo, where her brother was currently visiting.

"Because I had never imagined anything so beautiful." Maddie smiled as she remembered her first glimpse of the New Mexico sky, that vast, liberating sweep of endless brilliant blue, the lavender mountains in the distance, the open spaces of the desert. It was only there that she could finally breathe again. Where she had the space to be free. "And because I met you girls, and your mother and your brother and Uncle Gunther, and you were all the kindest people. I knew I could be at home here."

"What about your cousin? Is she a movie star?" Ruby asked.

Maddie glanced at Juanita. Gwen wasn't really a woman Juanita would approve of. Juanita always *tsk*ed about "flappers," and Gwen was certainly a flapperish sort of girl, with her love of parties and clothes and a good cocktail.

But Juanita also knew how Maddie and Gwen had once been like sisters when they were girls together in New York, and how Maddie worried because there hadn't been a letter from Gwen in some time.

And, aside from two small appearances in "dancing jazz babies" flicks, Gwen hadn't shown up on Santa Fe's small movie screen, either.

"No, not yet," Maddie answered. "It does sometimes take time to find the right part."

"Lilli Lamont was discovered drinking a root beer float at the Woolworth's counter," Pearl said. "Maybe your cousin should do that."

Maddie laughed. "Maybe so," she said, thinking the girls seemed to be reading too many movie gossip rags.

Ruby wrinkled her nose. "Floats are fattening. *Ladies' Circle* says so."

Yes. Definitely too many magazines. Maddie vowed to keep them more out of sight from then on.

"What nonsense," Juanita said briskly. "You two are always running and jumping so much, it would take a thousand floats to plump you up enough. And you know it's what in your hearts that counts. What you see in a movie is only a dream. You'll learn that with the Sisters and their school lessons."

Pearl and Ruby nodded, but they still looked doubtful.

"It's time to wash up for dinner," Juanita said. "You need to let Señora Maddie finish her dress. Dr. Cole will be here soon."

Juanita very much approved of Dr. Cole, ever since he had been of so much assistance when her husband Tomas died. Maddie liked the doctor, too, more than she wanted to admit. He made her smile and laugh, and feel all fluttery and nervous, in a girlish way she barely remembered. His blue eyes, his golden beard, his rare smile, his quiet kindness—he was a find indeed.

"Oh, yes, that reminds me," Maddie said, tying off the end of her thread and trying to push away those ridiculously dreamy thoughts. "I need your help with something, Juanita."

"What is that, Señora Maddie?"

Maddie lifted a strand of heavy, dark hair that had fallen from its pins. "I need you to bob my hair. It's time I joined the 1920s." She laughed at the appalled look on Juanita's face, and the twins clapped their hands in delight. "But I promise. There will be no peroxide."

CHAPTER 2

It was *her* painting. Maddie's very own work, hanging on a museum wall for everyone to see. She didn't quite know if she wanted to laugh—or be sick.

She studied the small oil scene, her own pink-brown adobe house and bright garden, a swirl of brilliant colors in the amber light of a late autumn afternoon. How she had struggled to capture that magical, shimmering light! One moment she had grown so frustrated that she'd even tossed her brushes to the ground, making Buttercup bark like it was all a fun game of "fetch the brushes." It still wasn't *quite* right, but a small red dot proclaimed it sold, so it was too late.

She glanced at her other work, an image of the distant mountains at sunset, the peaks all lavender and indigo-blue, touched with bits of snowy white against the broad sweep of gold and rose light. The quiet intensity, the solitude, of the hours she had spent working on it seemed very far away amid the noise and chaos of the party.

Ever since Maddie had arrived in Santa Fe, she had dreamed of having her work shown in the new Museum of Fine Arts. The building, one of the largest in town and on a prominent corner across from the Palace of the Governors, was only a few years old but looked as if it had always been there, with its rounded, pueblo-like walls, towers, and balconies. Inside, it was all dark wood floors and pale walls, covered with brilliant paintings, lined with glass cases filled with gorgeous pottery. And she was there, too, for everyone to see!

"Darling, there you are! Oh, look at your hair; aren't you just the bee's knees? About time you bobbed it," she heard a voice call, and she turned to see her friend Gunther Ryder pushing his way toward her through the crowd. Gunther was tall and slender, his pale features touched by his patrician New York Jewish background, his red hair grown back after the peroxide disaster and smoothed into a crest with Brylcreem. The green-and-white polka dot cravat she'd brought him back from her last journey to Manhattan gleamed as bright as his smile. He held two heavy pottery goblets, especially designed to go with the Pueblo Revival style of the new museum, and he pressed one into Maddie's hand. "Here, have some of this delicious planter's punch. Not much punch to it,

I'm afraid, but I did add a touch of my own special brew."

"Oh, Gunther, you are an angel," Maddie said, taking a sip of the deceptively sweet, fruity concoction. It was bracing, but she knew better than to imbibe *too* freely of Gunther's special brews. "I was feeling rather queasy just looking at my paintings here for anyone to see."

Gunther cocked his head to one side to study the mountains. "Maddie, my pet, you have nothing to fear. They're exquisite, so full of light and freedom! And you've sold one already, before the party even had time to really get started. I do understand, though."

Maddie thought of the rows of Gunther's past books, all best-selling romantic sagas—and the current story, which had been stalled in his typewriter for weeks. "Really, Gunther?"

"Of course. I've done book launch tours and read some really shocking reviews, which is never fun. But no one ever starts reading my stories right in front of me for a bit of on-the-spot critique. Not like you poor painters at openings like these. Think how hideous it must be for actors!"

Maddie laughed. "So true. No one has ever thrown rotten tomatoes at me, at least not in person."

"And they stand on stage night after night, facing that audience. I shudder to think about it. Oh, but speaking of actors, I just met the most fascinating person."

"An actor? Someone famous?" Maddie thought of small Santa Fe, barely five thousand people. Any actor at all who appeared on their streets, famous or not so much, would be an object of fascination. But once in a while they did see someone well known, usually come to take the cure at Sunmount Sanatorium.

"Not exactly famous, but close. He's a poet, someone I met once while I was on a book tour in California, but now he says he writes scenes for the movies. Quite a lucrative bit of business, it seems."

"Really? How fascinating!" Maddie remembered the stacks of movie mags in her kitchen, the twins pouring over photos of the Gishes and the Talmadges. They would love it if she could give them some behind-the-scenes details of moviemaking. "Is he here? Has he done any flicks I might have seen lately?" Their little theater didn't get *all* the newest films, but she tried to take the twins to see whatever came around.

Gunther studied the crowd over the rim of his goblet. "Oh, he's right over there, talking to your ever-so-dishy doctor. His name is William Royle. He's from New York, though I don't remember him from there. I think he's just started in the movie business. He's staying here with the Hendersons to do some work."

"Will Royle?" Maddie cried. But surely it couldn't be the same Will? The one whose parents had lived across the street from her own, who had played pranks with her in the park when they were children? Had danced with her at cotillion, taken her sledding in the winter, and even given her her very first kiss (though Peter had never known about that)? She well remembered his dark eyes, his constant laughter. She went up on tiptoe to study the faces around her.

She saw David Cole, the "dishy doctor," first, standing in the arched doorway that led down the stairs to the entrance hall. His golden hair, turning silver at the temples, gleamed in the light, and he was taller than almost everyone else, impossible to miss. He had been waylaid by some of his patients when they arrived and sent her a grimace as they were separated, but Maddie had just smiled and waved and left him to it.

In the short but wonderful time they had been friends, she had become accustomed to David's work. Not to mention accustomed to his dishy English accent. There were so few doctors in town, and none as handsome, charming, and deeply caring as David. He worked part of the week at Sunmount and part of the week in town, at St. Vincent's Hospital behind the cathedral, treating anyone who needed him.

He wasn't with his patients now, though. He was talking to William and Alice Henderson, leading members of society in Santa Fe and great patrons of the arts. With them was a man in a sharply tailored charcoal gray suit that could have come only from Gurjot in New York, his dark hair patent-leather smooth, his bright white smile flashing. If Maddie hadn't known him, she would almost have said he was Valentino himself. But she did know him. It really was her old friend Will Royle, after all those years.

She felt a sudden warm rush of longing, of nostalgia for laughter once had. For the excitement of being young.

"Jeepers," she whispered.

Gunther gave her a sharp glance. "*Do* you know him, darling?"

Maddie put on a bright smile, pushing away all those old, bittersweet memories. Thoughts of home as it had once been, too long ago. "Oh, yes. His family lives just across the street from mine, or they used to, until his mother's health meant they had to move south. We used to go sledding together in Central Park in the winter, and he taught me to ice skate. How extraordinary he should turn up here!"

Gunther frowned thoughtfully. "Sledding, eh? Fascinating."

David glanced at her just then, and Maddie waved at him.

"Should we go say hello?" Gunther said. "I'm quite aching to get to know this Mr. Royle a bit better!"

But before Maddie could answer, there was a sudden ripple of commotion at the entrance. The crowd seemed to shift, their heads turning toward the doorway.

A tiny figure burst through, like something escaped from a bizarre production of *A Midsummer Night's Dream.* Petite, fragile, with silvery-blonde hair cut in an Eton crop that revealed the elegant, sharp angles of high cheekbones, a pointed chin, a tiny nose. Her skin was paper-white, except for hectic spots of red in her cheeks.

Rather than wearing gossamer fairy robes, though, her blue tweed travel suit was rumpled, with a stain on the skirt. She spun in a frantic circle as everyone around stopped their conversation and stared in astonishment.

"Gwen!" Maddie gasped. A wave of relief broke over her—it had been so long since she'd heard from her cousin, and now here she was! But concern quickly followed, for Gwen looked like she was about to collapse. Maddie thrust her half-empty goblet at Gunther and rushed toward her cousin. "Gwen, what on earth are you doing here?"

"Maddie! Oh, Maddie. I've been looking for you everywhere in this forsaken town!" Gwen said with a ragged sob. She stumbled forward and fell into Maddie's arms. Maddie was appalled at how thin and frail Gwen felt, like a tiny, bony bird wrapped in Jicky-scented tweed. "Thank heaven I found you. I'm in such trouble . . ."

Chapter 3

"Will she be all right?" Maddie asked as she peered down at her cousin in worry. Gwen was sleeping after David gave her an injection, her elfin face as white as the linen pillows on Maddie's guest bed. Dark purple shadows looked like bruises under her closed eyes, and her hands were curled up like a child's against the blue nightdress borrowed from Maddie's closet.

She'd been able to say little as Maddie and David took her home from the museum, just sobbing and saying over and over that she had been "silly and stupid," that she was sorry. There seemed to be no trace of the bold, laughing girl who'd always led their childhood pranks.

She had only grown quiet when David gave her the sedative, and now she slept fitfully. Maddie glanced up from her cousin to study David's expression, hoping it would tell her something, but he just looked calm and solemn, his "caring doctor's bedside manner" face.

"I think so," he said. "I couldn't find anything wrong with her, though she'll have to come to the hospital for a proper exam. She just seems exhausted, and a bit malnourished."

Maddie gently touched Gwen's gaunt hand. "Poor girl."

David reached down to test Gwen's pulse. "When was the last time you saw her?"

Maddie tried to remember exactly. "Oh, ages ago. She was with me when I first came to Santa Fe after Pete died. We were going to California. I stayed here, and she went on. She always wanted to be an actress, you see. She was still in Los Angeles when I went back to New York a few months ago. Her mother didn't say much about her, but I do sometimes get letters from Gwen. She always sounds cheerful." Maddie carefully tucked the blankets closer around the sleeping girl. "I should have tried to get her to talk more. Maybe gone to see her in California. She was always so determined."

"I'm sure she'll tell you more in the morning. You should get some sleep now, Maddie. That injection will have her out for hours, and you're looking pale yourself. I don't want two new patients on my hands."

Maddie laughed softly. She thought of how hard he worked, the long hours at the hospital and out at Sunmount, the home visits. He never turned anyone in need away. "No, you're quite busy enough as it is. Come on,

David, I'll walk you out to the garden gate, and then I promise I'll get some sleep. It's been a too frightfully exciting night."

She took his arm and they made their way out of the quiet house. Only Buttercup waited by the door. Juanita, who had been sitting up reading movie mags when they brought in the sobbing Gwen, had left a plate of sandwiches and a pot of tea, and then at Maddie's urging had left for her own guesthouse to see to the girls. Juanita wouldn't pry or ask too many questions, no matter how curious she might actually be.

The night was soft and cool, full of the crisp hint of approaching autumn. Soon the mountainsides would be golden with the turning aspens, the days shorter, the air scented with pinon wood smoke and roasting green chilies.

Maddie rubbed at the nape of her neck as the wind brushed over her bare skin, surprised not to feel the old, familiar weight of heavy hair. She'd almost forgotten she'd cut it, previously the biggest excitement of the evening. It probably looked like a rumpled mess now.

She strolled slowly with David to her garden gate, letting the healing beauty of the sanctuary she had created for herself soothe her troubled, worried thoughts. The scent of the flowers on the night air, the soft rustle of the wind through the trees, the twinkle of the stars in the endless sky above made her feel calmer.

"Were you close to your cousin when you were girls?" David asked.

"Oh, yes," she answered, suddenly realizing she and David had never talked much about their pasts. They usually spoke of books and music, his work at the hospital, her painting, the people they knew in town. She knew his wife had died in the influenza epidemic, and that he was from Brighton, England, where his father and grandfather had both been doctors before him. He had been a medic in the same war that killed poor Pete, but he seldom mentioned it at all. She wondered if he had ever had cousins that were like siblings, too, or felt the tug of family ties even so far from home.

"I always just wanted to hide away and draw when we were children," she went on, leaning against the white-painted gate that divided her garden from Gunther's and the narrow, dusty lane beyond. Her friend's windows were dark now, but she was sure he would be wanting all the information in the morning. "Gwen was always so full of energy, so many mischievous ideas, pranks on our nannies, things like that. Once she brought her pony into the house and kept him in her mother's bathtub! We were sent off to Miss Spence's together, but she nearly got tossed out on the second day. Only the fact that her parents are Astors saved her, even after she lured the poor pony up the stairs a second time at school just before graduation."

David laughed. "That poor horse."

"Indeed. It livened up a drag of a geometry lesson, though. It wasn't surprising she wanted to be an actress. Our mothers were appalled. Acting was even worse than wanting to be a painter to them."

"Has she been in many flicks?"

"A couple that I know of, but only small parts. She used to say she would be Lady Macbeth one day, but I thought she would be better in funny parts. More Constance Talmadge than Norma, you know?" She remembered how Gwen had looked when she burst into the museum, so frantic, so pale, her face tearstained. She shivered. "I wonder what went wrong."

David frowned. "Could be a lot of things, I'm afraid. We do see movie types out at Sunmount quite a bit. Their directors send them out here to recover from, er, exhaustion."

Maddie remembered the bootleggers and worse she had met with when Juanita's husband was murdered. "Drugs?"

"Possibly. Or just worn down with work. It's not an easy job, for all everyone thinks it's so glamorous."

"No." Being artistic was never easy, Maddie thought. In order to paint or write or act, a person had to face life for what it was, beautiful and horrible and frightening all at once. To stay open to experience even when you just wanted to scream and run away. Add to that the pressures of fame, of staying beautiful and energetic, as a movie star had to do, and she was sure it could become unbearable.

Was that what had happened to sweet, funny, peppy Gwen? Maddie hoped not.

David gave her a reassuring smile and took her into his arms to press a soft, gentle kiss to her lips. Maddie felt the warmth, the hope, of his touch, and clung to him for a long moment. "Try to sleep, Maddie. I'll come to see your cousin tomorrow, if she would rather not come to the hospital, and then you and I can have our lunch date. A night's sleep will do you both good."

"Is that your professional prescription?" she teased.

"It definitely is."

She smiled up at him, his golden hair gilded in the moonlight, an elusive dimple in his sun-browned cheek as he gave her one of his rare smiles. "Then I'll do it. Good night, David."

After he left, she lingered in the garden for a while. It was a beautiful evening, the air cool as summer was sliding slowly into fall, and the stars seeming to actually glitter above her head. The soft scent of the flowers soothed and steadied her as she wandered past them.

She peeked in on Gwen before she went to her own bed. Gwen still slept, but she had tossed around in her dreams, the blankets heaped on the floor. Maddie carefully tucked them back around her frail shoulders and smoothed her rumpled, pale hair back from her brow. It felt warm, but Gwen settled back down into quiet slumber again.

"Oh, Gwen, my dear," Maddie whispered. "What has happened to you?"

CHAPTER 4

Maddie was up early the next morning, but as she made her way toward the kitchen, she could already hear voices there. A low hum of chatter, a burst of laughter. A quick glance into the guest room showed her that Gwen was already up, the bedclothes left in an untidy heap.

Maddie hurried into the kitchen and found Gwen sitting at the table with the twins while Juanita stirred a pot on the stove. The girls, already dressed for school in their new black-and-white uniforms, showed Gwen their treasured dolls, brought back by Maddie from New York. Gwen was braiding Ruby's long, black hair with a length of red ribbon.

Gwen was still pale, Maddie saw with a worried glance, but her hair was washed and brushed into a gleaming, silvery cap. The green trim of the dressing gown she wore, borrowed from Maddie, matched her eyes, which sparkled as she giggled with the girls.

"I used to braid Maddie's hair just like this when we were your age, and my own before I cut it," Gwen said. "But mine was never as thick and shiny as yours, girls. I do envy it."

"Yours is such a nice color, though," Pearl said, holding up her doll with the blonde braids and pink chiffon dress. "Like Lady Phoebe."

"You were the only one who was any good at fixing hair," Maddie said with a smile, as she poured herself a cup of coffee from the pot on the warmer.

Gwen looked up, her own smile deepening. She did look better this morning, her eyes clear, her smile calm, but Maddie didn't quite trust it. She remembered too well how distraught Gwen had been just yesterday, "Maddie, dearest! I *had* to learn to do my own coiffure. Nanny pulled so hard. Such a tyrant."

"Your nanny in your castle in New York?" Ruby said.

"Not really a castle," Gwen said, her smile fading into a small, wistful sadness. "Just a large, gloomy, cold crypt. Nothing like your lovely house here, all full of color and light. Maddie was always the best at creating beauty wherever she went. It just seems to follow her around, like a sunbeam. I always knew she would be a great artist."

Maddie smiled, remembering those long-ago days of

hiding in the attic with Gwen, the two of them drawing and reading for hours, talking of what they would do and be one day. "And I always knew you would be a great actress," she said, sitting down at the table.

Gwen tied off the end of Ruby's ribbon, her Cupid's-bow lips turned down at the corners. "Not so great. I've never been a lucky person like you, Maddie. I'm always making the wrong decisions. Taking the wrong path."

Juanita gave Maddie a questioning glance, a small nod. She put the lid on the simmering pot and held out her hands to her daughters. "Come along, *niñas*, let's find your school satchels or you'll be late on your very first day."

"Will you walk us to school, Señora Maddie?" Pearl asked. "You said you would, so we wouldn't be nervous."

Maddie looked uncertainly at Gwen, who gave a bright smile and a little wave of her hand. "Oh, yes, Maddie, you must! I would hate to think I messed up any of your plans with my silliness. I should probably take a little nap this morning, get some rest like that handsome doctor said."

"And eat some breakfast, Señorita Astor," Juanita said, her motherliness unstoppable. She always looked after everyone around her.

"Of course I will, Mrs. Anaya," Gwen answered. "This omelet looks too scrumptious for words."

But when Juanita and the twins went out the back

door, headed to their guesthouse at the back of the garden, Gwen just picked at the plate in front of her, not looking up at Maddie. Maddie poured herself another cup of coffee and sat down to wait.

"Gwen, darling, you are absolutely *not* messing up any of my plans," she said. She longed to reach out to touch her cousin's hand, but something about Gwen's still, quiet sadness, her invisible distance, held her back. "It's wonderful to see you again. But what has happened? Please let me help you."

Gwen glanced up fleetingly with a flash of that overly bright smile. "Maddie, you always have been the dearest of dears. I've just been such a silly-billy lately. I don't know what came over me."

Maddie thought of how Gwen had looked last night, frantic and tearstained. "It must have been something serious to bring you all this way." Santa Fe was a far jaunt from anywhere, the train station miles away in Lamy.

Gwen gave a dismissive wave. "Oh, I'm here for work! That's all."

"Work?" Maddie said doubtfully.

"Yes. I got a part in a movie they're filming here. A cowboy flick. *The Far Sunset*. Isn't that utterly marvelous?"

"A movie? Here in New Mexico?"

"Yes, a Western. It's not exactly Shakespeare, just a story about a family coming West in a covered wagon to homestead, being menaced by Indians and dust storms and romantic jealousy, that sort of thing. I play Tillie, the family's maid. A small but intense part; she's nearly kidnapped by mountain ruffians. They're shooting interiors later in California, at the studio, but they wanted some real on-site exteriors to add a bit of authenticity. Luther Bishop is directing, and his wife is starring."

"Luther Bishop?" Maddie said.

"You've heard of him?"

"Of course. There's only one little theater here in town, but Juanita and I like to read about all the stars in *Photoplay* and *Movie Magic*. Luther Bishop is famous after *The Lady X*. And he's married to Bridget Bishop, so glamorous. I can't believe they're coming to Santa Fe."

"Yes." Gwen looked away, poking her fork at her congealing eggs. "Terribly glamorous. I don't think they're here just yet, though, at least not in town. There was some sort of trouble out at the Henderson ranch, where they're building most of the sets. We've had to move filming, though I think the Hendersons are still investing in the film."

"The Hendersons were loaning Mr. Bishop their ranch?" William and Alice Henderson, he an architect and she a well-known poet, were great patrons of the arts in Santa Fe, always involved in various cultural projects, but she hadn't heard of them letting anyone use their ranch outside town, or their large adobe hacienda near the plaza.

Gwen shrugged. "I suppose they were. Luther can charm whatever he wants out of anyone."

Maddie gave her a sharp glance, a sudden suspicion moving over her like a cold chill. "Gwen—do your troubles have anything to do with this Mr. Bishop?"

Gwen looked away, but not before Maddie glimpsed tears in her eyes. Her slender shoulders hunched. "Oh, Maddie. I was really so dumb. He's so handsome, so funny and smart, the most talented director in town. Everyone says so. I loved him, and I thought he loved me. He swore he and Bridget hadn't been *really* married in years, that he wanted me, and would marry me and make me a movie star. But it turned out he told that to lots of girls."

Maddie thought it sounded like the plot of a movie melodrama—one where everyone ended up dead for their sins at the end. She reached out to grab Gwen's trembling hands and held on to them tightly, her heart breaking for her fragile cousin. "Oh, Gwen. What a cad! I am so sorry." A seed of a startled thought took hold, and Maddie glanced down at Gwen's flat midriff. "You aren't . . ."

Gwen cringed, and pulled back to wrap the folds of the dressing gown closer. "No! I—I thought I might be. I told Luther, and he—he told me to take care of it. That he would give me the money, and make sure I got a good movie part once it was over. Luckily, a doctor friend of mine, a woman, told me I was mistaken. I had just lost so much weight my monthlies stopped. It's been hard to eat."

Maddie was shocked and appalled. "What happened with Mr. Bishop, then?"

Gwen sniffled. "I used his money for a new car, but I crashed it on Mulholland Drive after a party. And he only gave me this pathetic little part. He said Bridget would get mad if the lead went to someone else besides her."

"Gwen. You poor, darling lamb." Maddie stood up to take her cousin into her arms, holding her close as Gwen sobbed her heart out, as she obviously had needed to do for a long time. Maddie understood heartbreak, the pain of loss that followed a person around and ached and ached, like a missing limb. Nothing could fill that hollow, nothing but time and care. "You can't stay on with that movie when the Bishops get here. Why don't you just stay with me for a while? You wouldn't believe the wonderful peace of the mountains here . . ."

Gwen drew back and stared up at Maddie with horror written on her tear-streaked face. "I have to stay with the movie! It's my best chance to be noticed, to get better parts. I don't care about that jerk Luther now, or his jealous witch of a wife. I just need to finish the part. Rex Neville is the leading man. It's sure to be a big hit!"

Before Maddie could answer, could try to make sense of it all, the twins came running back into the kitchen,

their knapsacks heavy with books and their mother following them, trying to get them to put on their jackets.

"Señora Maddie, you said you would walk us to
school!" Pearl clamored. Ruby nodded in agreement.

"Girls, I told you—Señora Maddie has a guest," Juanita scolded.

Gwen swiped at her eyes and then gave them a brilliant smile. She seemed utterly transformed from the sor-
row of a moment before, and Maddie thought maybe she
really did belong in movies. "No, Mad-catkins, you go to
school with these lovely girls, and then do whatever you
usually do during the day. I don't want to be in the way."

Juanita gave Maddie a long glance, one that promised
she would stay close to Gwen. And David had said he
would look in that morning, too. "You go ahead, Señora
Maddie. Señorita Astor has told me she will tell me all
about working with Lillian Gish." Lillian was Juanita's
favorite.

But Maddie was still unsure. "I don't know . . ."

"Aren't you supposed to have a late breakfast at La
Fonda with Dr. Cole?" Juanita asked. Ever since David
had helped Juanita after her husband's death, he could do
no wrong in her eyes.

"Dr. Cole?" Gwen said, perking up as she always had at
the first hint of romantic gossip. "That ever-so-handsome
man who brought us home last night? I may have been a

bit lally-do, but I certainly remember him. Is he your new beau?"

Maddie felt her cheeks turn warm as she remembered their good-night kiss, and she turned away to rinse out her coffee cup. "I wouldn't say that exactly."

Gwen gave a mischievous grin. "I can see now why you wouldn't want to go back to New York. My mother is always writing and complaining that she and Aunt Vaughn have such terribly ungrateful daughters who won't do their duties."

"They want us both to come back to New York so much?"

"Of course they do. But that sort of life has never been for the likes of us, has it? We always wanted more from life."

"No," Maddie murmured. "It never was for us."

CHAPTER 5

The twins chattered happily as Maddie walked them to school through the streets just starting to come alive for the day. They were narrow and winding, old donkey trails that had sprung up when Santa Fe was a Spanish settlement, all dusty adobe, and now they had barely been widened for carts and motorcars. Shop doors were opening, window shades going up, and wagons full of groceries being delivered from Kaune's and the dairy rattled past.

The twins tugged at Maddie's hands, and begged to stop for barley twists and jelly beans at the candy store, and asked question after question about Maddie's New York childhood with Gwen. Only once they turned the corner and were within sight of the school, with its cream-colored stone and slate mansard roof in a French style that stood out from all the tan and pale pink adobe, did they suddenly become silent. Their feet dragged a bit in their new patent-leather Mary Janes.

Maddie wasn't entirely sure she blamed them. The school looked formal, European, enclosed in a wrought-iron fence, all silent elegance. The chapel next to it, a small jewel box of stained glass and gray stone, was crowned with a tall statue of Mary that seemed to peer down, all-seeing, over the girls going up the school steps. It was rather intimidating, reminding her of all the nervous-making first days at Miss Spence's.

But the Sister who stood outside the doors ringing the summoning bell looked friendly, rosy-cheeked under her starched white wimple, the other girls who dashed past in their matching uniforms giggling and eager. The second nun with her was a bit younger and had a sweet, shy smile.

"I'm sure you will have such a jolly time today," Maddie said, squeezing the girls' hands and giving them a bright smile. "There's all the wonderful books you'll read, and the other girls you'll meet! You'll be able to tell Eddie all about it when he gets home from your uncle's next month. And we can have cake this afternoon."

"Chocolate?" Pearl asked doubtfully.

"Oh, yes. Your mother has everything all ready to mix up. It will be just like your birthday."

"Well. Maybe we can give school a try . . ." Ruby said.

"This must be Ruby and Pearl!" the older Sister called

out, seeming to sense when pupils were a bit reluctant. "Father Malone has told us all about you. I'm Sister Mary Cecilia, and you'll be in my own class this year. This is my assistant, Sister Angelica. We have two special desks all picked out for you."

Maddie let go of their hands and watched them march up the steps with a little pang in her heart. She remembered when she had been their age, going to school hand in hand with Gwen, marching up the stone steps into a chalk-scented classroom. The fear of the new, stepping out of childhood into girlhood. It was hard to watch the girls do the same, though she did hope school in Santa Fe was different from New York, calmer, more casual, more welcoming. She smiled and waved as they glanced back one last time, and she tried not to start crying.

As Sister Mary Cecilia closed the doors, Maddie turned toward La Fonda Hotel at the end of the street. She thought more about her own schooldays in New York with Gwen. What mischief her cousin had led them into back then! It seemed like they were always laughing when they were together. What had happened to Gwen since then? How had it gone wrong?

She pushed through the heavy carved doors into the lobby at La Fonda and took a deep breath of the familiar scents of beeswax polish, leather upholstery, and green chilies from the restaurant. It was her favorite gathering place, as it was for the rest of the townspeople, and she always felt better when she stepped into the familiar, pale golden light. It was all so airy and elegant, built to look like a Spanish hacienda around an open courtyard, the painted glass windows letting in the bright sun. There was always someone to talk to there, lounging on the settees and cushioned chairs, sipping tea on the portal.

She waved at Anton, the frighteningly efficient Swiss concierge who ruled the hotel, and made her way toward the restaurant at the back of the building. It was darker, cozier, the walls painted with colorful murals, the tables tucked into nooks and corners, the air filled with the quiet hum of laughter and the delicious smells of fine cuisine.

"Maddie," David said, jumping up to hold out her chair for her. He didn't look at all as if he had stayed up with a sobbing patient into the wee hours. His blue eyes were bright, his hair a shining guinea-gold, his smile flashing from his short-trimmed beard. "How is your cousin this morning? I will check on her later today."

"Better, I think. She was out of bed and eating breakfast when I left," she answered. She decided not to tell him about what had brought Gwen to Santa Fe: the movie, the unhappy affair. That was her cousin's own secret. But she did hope to persuade Gwen to talk to David about her weight loss, which was a worry. "Speaking of which, I am utterly famished! I just dropped the twins off for their first day of school with the Sisters of Loretto, and I feel rather melancholy about it all."

David gave her an understanding smile. "They are growing up."

"Much too fast." As the waiter brought coffee and muffins, they chatted about the girls and about memories of their own schooldays, and for a few minutes Maddie forgot her worries about her cousin.

Then she noticed Elizabeth Grover coming into the restaurant, dressed much too brightly for the morning hour in a short-skirted red suit and raven-feather trimmed cloche hat. Elizabeth was also a refugee from the East who had landed in Santa Fe, but she didn't paint or write. She was one of those black sheep of good families who would rather have them out of sight, and Maddie knew she was often involved in affairs with married senators and other government bigwigs. Maddie had even seen her with cocaine more than once. Elizabeth waved merrily and called out to a table full of people Maddie didn't recognize. Elizabeth dashed to the corner booth, and for an instant her bright hair and even brighter, frantic laughter reminded Maddie of Gwen, and made her worry even more.

She studied the people Elizabeth was meeting and saw they were as well dressed as she was, a couple of women with shingled hair in Chanel and men in sharply cut suits. Movie people, maybe?

"Gwen told me the most interesting thing," Maddie said. "She's in town to make a film! I didn't realize we were part of such a glamorous business here in our little desert paradise, though cowboy flicks do seem quite popular lately. William Hart, wagon trains, things like that."

"Oh, yes," David answered. "One of my colleagues at the hospital said an actress had come in yesterday, afraid she was coming down with a cold. Bridget something. Turned out she wasn't, but he gave her some cough syrup and got her autograph. Nurse Johnson said that when this lady left, she saw someone lurking outside the gates who looked like some famous gossip columnist, who apparently wears very strange hats. I hope we're not going to be invaded."

Maddie laughed, but in her mind she wondered if it was the famous Bridget Bishop, Luther's wife, who had come in to the hospital. Did she really just have a cold? "I'm afraid we might. I'm sure a movie needs oodles of people working on it, and this is the only nice hotel in town." She glanced again at the table in the corner. "Do you suppose those could be movie folk? They do look terribly glamorous."

He studied them with a wry smile. "I'm afraid I'm not the one to ask. I don't have the time to see many flicks. I doubt I would recognize any but the most famous. Mary Pickford, maybe, with the curls. None of them seem to be the gossip columnist, though. Their hats are much too small."

Their meals arrived then, and they dove into the food

and talked about the party at the museum, Maddie's plans for new paintings, David's work out at Sunmount. The pleasant hour passed too quickly, and all too soon they had to leave the cozy restaurant. The table of possible movie people still sat there, their laughter growing louder, Elizabeth's voice fluting above the others.

Maddie took David's arm as they stepped past the carved double doors and onto the street, the tall, square towers of the cathedral at the end of the lane turning golden as the brilliant sunlight climbed overhead. Behind the church's garden was the hospital, a white, three-story stone Victorian building that always seemed to have an air of efficiency and briskness about it. At the gate, David kissed her cheek and promised to call on Gwen as soon as he finished his rounds.

Maddie found she didn't want to go home quite yet. It was a beautiful day, the light so brilliant as it filtered through the tall trees of the garden, the breeze soft, promising the autumn soon to come. She decided to stop by the post office and see if the art supplies she had ordered from New York had arrived yet. It was hard to obtain all she needed in Santa Fe, and she was really eager to start new works after the success at the museum.

She crossed the plaza, sleepy at that time of day. A few elderly men sat on the wrought-iron benches in the shade, gossiping, watching the ladies hurry past on their shopping errands. Two large, wolflike dogs slept on the patches of grass near the bandstand, barely even glancing up as children stopped to pet them. She waved at the men, skirted around the tall stone war memorial obelisk at the center of the pathways, and turned toward the post office. The line wasn't long at that time of day, and it didn't take long for her to retrieve her package. She smiled down at the return address—Norbert and Sons, Fine Art Supplies, New York. Now she could really get to work!

"Madeline Vaughn?" she heard someone call as she tucked her package under her arm and straightened her hat. "Is that really you?"

She spun around to see a man hurrying toward her across the marble lobby, grinning as he held out his hand. He was tall and lean in his well-cut tan suit, his dark hair glossy and curling under his panama hat. His chocolate-colored eyes sparkled.

"William Royle?" she gasped. So it *had* been him at the museum, and he was just as handsome, as full of fizzy life, as he had been when they skated on the icy pond in Central Park so long ago. "Jeepers! Don't you look ever so lovely?"

"Not half as lovely as you," he said with a teasing lilt to his voice. He swept off his hat and carelessly pushed back the hair that fell boyishly over his brow. "I remember my mother wrote to me that you had moved out here to the middle of nowhere, and that your parents were prostrate with worry."

Maddie rolled her eyes. "So my mother tells me, all the time. But she needn't worry; I am doing very well here in the middle of nowhere. What are *you* doing here?" It was amazing, two figures from her past appearing in the same day.

"Oh, I'm writing," he said.

"Poetry again? I remember you won those prizes. Santa Fe is certainly wonderful for inspiration!"

He laughed ruefully, looking down at the hat he was spinning between his hands. "No, I had the most terrible block last year, and haven't pushed past it yet. I'm a scenarist for the movies at the moment. Filthy lucre and all that. I was out in New Jersey for a while, but now I live in California."

Now it all made sense. *"The Far Sunset?"*

"How did you know?"

"My cousin Gwendolyn is acting in it. As the maid, I think," Maddie said, wondering how much he knew about Gwen's predicament. Surely Hollywood was as rife with gossip as Santa Fe. But she couldn't tell from his expression, which never wavered from his smile. "She was staying with me last night."

"Gwen? How is she? I did see her once or twice around the stylish watering holes in Los Angeles, but she seemed to vanish for a while. I guess she was coming to see you. I haven't met any of the actors out here yet. I'm glad to hear she'll be on the set. What a fizz she is!"

"Yes. She is that." Maddie wondered what gossip Will could give her, what everyone might be saying about Luther Bishop. "I'm quite aching to know more about what the film world is really like."

Someone brushed past her, almost making her drop her package, and she realized they were blocking the doorway into the post office. Will gave her a rueful smile and offered her his arm, leading her out into the day.

Will clapped his dashing straw hat onto his glossy curls, tugging it low to block the blinding sunshine after the shadows of the post office. "This movie is an interesting piece, based on a novel I'm not sure anyone has read. It's been a pip to adapt. Luther Bishop is directing. Have you heard of him? He's had hit after hit lately."

Maddie thought of Gwen, the tears in her eyes, the despair of last night. "I've heard of him a bit."

"Well, he made piles of money for the Meyer Studio with *Jazz Babies* and *The Lady X* earlier this year, and now he wants to do something more prestigious. He decided a Western epic was just the thing, like *The Wagon Train*, but he didn't think a cramped studio was quite grand enough. So he decided to come out here to film the exteriors. All your mountains and deserts, a few real Indians as extras."

"Sounds fascinating. How did you come to get the job?"

They crossed the street onto the plaza, still sleepy and slow in the afternoon light. "I've been doing mostly

Charleston baby–type things lately and was getting tired of it, and there's this girl I've been sort of seeing. Lorelei Fontaine. She'd been hired as wardrobe designer on this Bishop project, though what she really wants to do is act."

"Of course," Maddie murmured. So many young women with ambitions just like Gwen.

"She got me the interview with Luther. We thought if I could make a bit of a name for myself on a prestige project like this, next year I could write Lorelei some big, sparkly vehicle. Make our way ahead at the studio."

"Sounds like she's lucky to have you."

He gave a rueful laugh, and to Maddie's surprise he even blushed a little. "Oh, we're not too serious. We just work well together. You've got to have lots of friends to get ahead in this business. I like a girl a little more— intellectual. There's lot of fluttery actresses around Los Angeles, but not too many with good heads on their shoulders."

He gave Maddie a long, intent look, and she looked away, flustered. "And this project is a Western, you say? Like Hart, or Tom Mix?"

"Bigger than that. It's got a really complicated plot, lots of complex characters, big settings. Bridget Bishop, Luther's wife, and Rex Neville are the stars."

"I saw Mr. Neville in *Sinners of the Streets* last time I was in New York! He was very good. So handsome, too."

"Harry Kelly was meant to do *Sunset*, revive his career

a bit, but they say he got sick last minute. Drink, I would imagine."

"Really?" She remembered Harry Kelly; he had been a stage actor before turning to film, and his Hamlet had been the talk of Broadway when she was a girl. She and Gwen had seen it three times, sighing over his dark good looks and intense charm. It was sad to think of all that talent wasted.

"Happens to lots of those old stars. But Rex stepped in, and he's better suited for the part anyway."

Maddie stumbled on a loose cobblestone, and this time her package fell to the ground with a clunk. "Oh, no," she gasped, hoping the precious supplies weren't damaged. "My paints!"

Will scooped it up for her, his long fingers running gently over the brown paper package. "Doesn't seem broken. Have you been working on your art again?"

"Yes, I even had some pieces in an exhibit at the art museum over there." She gestured to the large adobe building on the corner, its rounded, pale-brown walls and towers glowing. Students hurried up the steps, wrapped easels under their arms.

"That's wonderful, Maddie! I remember a painting your parents had on their dining room wall in New York. That garden in Florence. It was amazing. I'd never seen anything like it before. I couldn't believe a friend of mine had done it."

Maddie smiled with a warm glow of pleasure. "I told you it's inspiring here, for all sorts of art. Maybe you'll feel like composing a few new poems soon."

"It's movies for me for a while. It's what I get paid for. Hey, you might even want to try a bit of art direction for a flick or two? It's good fun, and they need talented people like you. Audiences are getting even pickier about how everything looks. They want beauty and authenticity."

Maddie laughed. "Me? Do movie sets? I don't know . . ."

"They would be lucky to have you! I tell you what—a fellow named Henderson is giving a party for us tomorrow."

"William Henderson? Everyone in Santa Fe knows the Hendersons. They're quite the patrons of the arts."

"He's invested a nice bit of change in the movie. Everyone will be at this 'do—Luther, Bridget, Rex, and my Lorelei, too. You should come and meet them all. I'll pick you up! Bring your Santa Fe friends!"

Maddie laughed at his enthusiasm. That hadn't changed about him at all. "Oh, Will. You can't just invite the whole town to someone else's party."

He gave her a cheeky grin. "Of course I can; the more, the merrier. Say you'll come. We can catch up. It'll be fun."

Maddie thought about it. She did like the Hendersons, and maybe she could help Gwen in some way if she got to know more about these movie people. "All right. But only for an hour or two."

"Smashing! Seven o'clock tomorrow? It seems like you Santa Fe sorts are early-to-bed types. What's your address?" He took the card she dug out of her handbag and kissed her cheek. "I have to run now, but see you tomorrow. It's wizard seeing you again, Mads, it really is."

Maddie watched him hurry off across the plaza, a burst of zipping, colorful energy in the quiet, lazy space. He seemed to make even the air around him pop and shimmer. She had to smile at the old memories of their childhood together. It *was* good to see him again, to remember happy times.

She suddenly glimpsed someone else at the edge of the low iron fence around the plaza, a plump lady in flowered silk, wearing an enormous hat covered with a spill of red and gold chrysanthemums, unlike any Maddie had ever seen. The woman darted off after Will, her face concealed by the deep brim of that astonishing hat. Maddie wondered if that was the famous gossip columnist who had been seen lurking outside the hospital. Why would she be following Will?

Maddie shrugged, and hurried on her own way toward home, worried about Gwen. She felt terrible for leaving her alone all morning, but when she reached her own sitting room, she saw Gwen looked far better than she had even a few hours ago. Maybe *too* good? Her eyes were as bright and hard as diamonds, her cheeks spotted with red as she dug through a large trunk in the middle of the red-and-gray woven Navajo rug. Piles of filmy, bright, silky clothes and heaps of shoes were strewn around on the carved Spanish furniture.

"Oh, Mad-catkins, there you are! My trunk arrived from the train station; isn't it marvelous? Now I won't look like an urchin in that old suit." Gwen held up a dress of Nile-green satin embroidered with gold and silver beads. "What do you think? It's Paquin. Maybe we can go out dancing tonight? Is there anywhere to go dancing here?"

"One or two spots, but you should rest, Gwen," Maddie said. She picked up an ermine-trimmed silver lamé cloak and held it up to the light. It didn't look like the sort of thing a struggling actress would have. But then there was Astor money, too.

"Oh, pooh, I feel fine! I just needed a bit of sleep, and some of your wonderful Juanita's delightful cooking," Gwen said. She held the gown up to her slim shoulders and twirled around. "I have to get to work soon, you know."

"Work? Gwen, surely you don't mean to go back to the movie."

Gwen held up a silver, double-strapped dancing shoe. "Of course I will. If I run away, I'll never get another part like this. I can't overreact to things and get a reputation for flightiness, not until I'm as big as Gloria Swanson."

Maddie knew when she couldn't argue with Gwen. Her cousin had that stubborn gleam in her green eyes, the gleam that said she would never listen to a word that contradicted what she wanted at that very moment. Maddie could only do her best to protect Gwen without letting her cousin know she was doing it. She had to stick as close to Gwen as she could.

"You'll never guess who I saw in town," Maddie said brightly, folding a stack of silk, lace-trimmed slips.

"Who?"

"Will Royle. Just as handsome as when we were kids. He said he's working as a writer on the movie."

"Will? How splendid! If the writers are in town, that must mean shooting is about to start. Did he say anything about it?"

"Not much."

"Isn't he just a doll, though? Everyone in LA is in love with him." Gwen shot Maddie a long glance from under her lashes. "He always did like you a lot."

Maddie shook her head. "We were just friends. He asked me to a party tomorrow, though."

"A party for the movie?" Gwen's tone went sharp and spiky with sudden anxiety.

"It sounds like it. At the Hendersons'. Will said they

had invested in the movie. He thinks I should try to do some art direction for the films or some such nonsense."

"He's absolutely right. You would be fabulous at it, and when I'm a big star you should design all my magnificent sets. Costumes, too. It will all make me even bigger than that stuck-up Norma Talmadge!" Gwen laughed merrily and held up a red satin dress. "Should I wear this one to the party? It's the most eye-catching thing I have. Or maybe the silver brocade? Is it more dignified for a real actress?"

Maddie wanted to argue, to insist that Gwen remain home, rest, stay far away from Luther Bishop. But she knew when it was futile to argue with her cousin. She could only stay close to her and try to protect her in any way possible.

CHAPTER 6

The house was lit up like a beacon as Will's car rolled to a stop on its curved, gravel driveway behind a line of other vehicles parked haphazardly around a stone fountain. It was a large house, an old hacienda the Hendersons had enlarged and modernized while still keeping the charming Spanish flavor in the mullioned windows and the tiled fountain at the center of the driveway. Every window was bright gold, the sound of music and laughter floating out the doorways.

"I say," Gwen giggled as Will helped her from the back seat. "This is really not too shabby. Mother and Aunt Vaughn are always talking like you all live in tepees out here, not even any running water or electric lights!" She swirled her beaded eau de nil gown into place and straightened her feathered headband on her short, platinum hair.

"No one ever lived in tepees out here, anyway. They

live in adobe pueblos," Maddie answered. She was getting awfully tired of that silly assumption! Every visitor seemed to make it, along with bemoaning the lack of eagle-feather headdresses and chuck wagons. "The pueblos look quite a bit like this house, actually, with flat roofs and curved walls, the windows and gates painted turquoise."

"How disappointing! I'm sure William here is going to refuse to put any tepees in the story now. He's such a stickler for authenticity!" She gave Will's cheek a pat and dashed ahead into the house. She seemed completely recovered now, jumping around with enthusiastic laughter as she always had.

Will offered Maddie his arm with a rueful smile, and they made their way into the party. "I *am* a stickler, you know, especially on historical flicks like this one. Once you know the truth about a period, you can't just ignore it."

"And it's a very good thing to be, surely? Artists should always strive for authenticity in their work."

"Tell that to the directors! They're always in a hurry. If you don't do eight or ten pictures in a year, you can't keep up with distributor demand. There are some, like Mr. Griffith, who care about every detail. Most just want to crank them out, make a buck, and move on."

"And which sort is this Luther Bishop?"

Will frowned thoughtfully. "He's all right, especially on this project. He wants to show he can do serious drama. Those glossy jazz-baby flicks he's mostly known for don't need much research, just big sets and fancy costumes, plenty of pretty girls."

"A family saga Western historical seems an odd choice for him, then."

"They say Walter Henschel was set to do it. He does those big, serious twelve-reelers all the time. But the studio gave it to Luther for some reason."

Maddie remembered what he had told her before. "Like how Rex Neville replaced Harry Kelly in the lead role?"

Will shrugged. "People get replaced all the time on projects. It's never a sure thing until it's in the can."

"What a stressful way to work."

"An artist never has much certainty. You know that, Mads."

"Oh, yes," she murmured. "I certainly know that."

They stepped into the foyer, a small, welcoming space with whitewashed walls trimmed in blue-and-white Portuguese tile with blue, gray, and red Navajo rugs on the wooden floor that spoke of the Hendersons' good taste and interest in local crafts. A butler stepped forward to take Maddie's satin evening coat, and she handed it over with a smile. She glanced in a silver-framed mirror and smoothed her bronze-colored satin gown, her wind-blown hair pinned back with her grandmother's pearl combs. She still hadn't quite gotten used to its cool, short length.

"So you know these people, Maddie?" Will asked as she straightened his tie. "The Hendersons?"

"Everyone in Santa Fe knows them," she answered. "He's an architect and artist, and she's a well-known poet. They came here years ago looking for a cure for Alice's tuberculosis, and decided to stay. They travel quite a bit, so I don't know them very well, but I've been to parties here once or twice, and have drinks with them at La Fonda sometimes."

"La Fonda?"

"The hotel across from the plaza. Everyone tends to congregate there; it's so welcoming and fun."

"Oh, yeah. I think everyone is staying there, but I'm at the De Vargas." He gave her a grin, his teeth flashing bright white. "I can see I need to stick with you, Mads, if I need a guide to the in-places around here."

Maddie smoothed the satin lapel of his evening jacket. "Not for long, you won't. Everyone will want to meet the handsome movie guy and get written into your next flick."

He preened a bit, twisting his head from side to side as if to display a matinee idol profile. "You think I'm handsome, then?"

Maddie laughed. "You always have been, and well

you know it! Now, should we go in, see who's here? I have to admit, I'm awfully excited about meeting some movie people myself."

"I promise, you won't be so excited for long. They're all dull as tombs, never talk about anything but themselves."

The butler showed them into the party space, a large atrium at the back of the house. The windows were open to let in the cool air, since there were crowds of people on the adobe window seats, gathered on couches, dancing in the sitting room.

Maddie took a glass of champagne from a tray a maid was passing around and studied the crowd. She saw several people she knew, waving to Olive Rush, the artist, tall and distinctive in her velvet Navajo skirt and brightly printed turban, and at Gunther who was chatting with a group across the room. She had completely lost sight of Gwen.

She also recognized a man who could only be the actor Rex Neville. He wasn't as tall as she had expected, being rather lean and compact, but she had never seen anyone so unhumanly handsome. He looked like a Renaissance painting rather than a real person, with a face sharply carved in planes and angles, a noble brow, and pale-blue eyes that contrasted beautifully with his dark, waving hair. She itched to paint him.

He stood in the corner near the phonograph, a large tumbler of amber-colored whiskey in his hand as he whispered intently with the lady at his side. She was also quite petite, delicate and fine-boned with strawberry-blonde, spun-sugar hair pinned atop her head and fastened with a gold leaf-shaped clip, and an ultra-stylish cream-and-gold chiffon gown. She shook her head, making her diamond chandelier earrings shimmer, and took a sip of champagne.

"There's Lorelei," Will said, gesturing to the lady in chiffon.

"Your girlfriend, the wardrobe designer?" Maddie asked, surprised. She had thought surely the lady must be an actress, from her looks and bored demeanor, and that she must be with Rex.

Will laughed. "Not exactly my girlfriend. Just a convenient relationship, personally and professionally. You understand."

Maddie wasn't sure she did. But then, she had read enough fan magazines to know movie people were *different*. "Sure," she murmured. "So, that's Rex Neville she's talking to. He's certainly young, and gorgeous. More—compact than I would have expected."

"Movie actors are often on the smallish side. Easier to cast, more limber, fits better in the sets. You see, there's Bridget Bishop over there. Five feet in her high heels, but a stunner."

Maddie turned to look at the woman who was talking to the Hendersons near the French doors that led out to the garden. She *was* a stunner, with a heart-shaped face framed with a sleek blonde bob, her eyes large and vividly green, her laugh a silvery trill that matched her lamé dress. "My goodness. I didn't know people could look like that in real life."

"I know, right?" Will said with a chuckle. "I nearly fell on my keister when I first saw her."

"I'd love to paint her portrait. Her features are so elegant, so symmetrical, and her coloring is wonderful."

"She'd surely let you. Like most actors, she loves having her picture done. But I warn you—her conversation never quite matches her exterior."

"How so?"

"She's an Irish convent school girl from Brooklyn. She likes to curse a lot. She knows a lot of words I'd never heard before. Complains a lot, too."

"Oh, well. I'm very good at tuning things out while I'm painting. And I'm in need of some good new curse words." Maddie sipped at her champagne, which was very good, French if she wasn't mistaken, and continued to study the crowd around them. She waved at some friends and wondered who the strangers were. "And where is the famous Luther Bishop?"

William scanned the party with a frown. "I don't see him anywhere. I hope he hasn't already pulled his vanishing act."

"Vanishing act?"

"At parties and nightclubs, he always disappears for a good chunk of the evening with some chorus girl or cocktail waitress."

"With his wife right there?"

"Sure. He's not usually gone so early, though, and not when there are rich patrons around."

"I doubt there are many chorus girls or cocktail waitresses here."

William laughed, a sound with a bit of a bitter tang to it. "Oh, he'll find one somewhere."

Maddie was suddenly even more worried about having lost Gwen in the crowd. Will was called away by one of his friends, and Maddie took another glass of champagne before she wandered around the edge of the party, watching the people. It was a colorful lot; it seemed like everyone in town was there.

At last she caught a glimpse of Gwen's green dress. Her cousin was chatting with Rex Neville and Lorelei Fontaine by the phonograph, sorting through the records. Gwen was smiling happily and waved at Maddie.

Maddie waved back, and took a few minutes while Gwen was occupied to study the paintings on the walls and displayed on easels. Mountain landscapes and Native portraits from the Taos artists, mixed with a few Impressionists and even a Flemish still life or two. To her surprise, she suddenly found herself facing something very familiar—her own mountain scene from the museum exhibit.

"I do hope you don't mind that we were the ones who bought it, Mrs. Alwin," Alice Henderson said, appearing at Maddie's side with a bright pink cocktail in her hand. Alice was a pretty woman, with soft brown eyes, dark hair piled atop her head, and a fashionable dark-red gown with draped sleeves and a fringed hem. Her smile was warm and welcoming. "You captured the feeling of the storm coming over the mountains so wonderfully."

"Of course I don't mind," Maddie answered. "I'm terribly flattered to be here on the wall with Mr. Sharp and Mr. Blumenschein!"

"Tell me, what are you working on now?"

"I just finished a couple of portraits and have started on a new landscape. The Pedernal peak, out by Abiquiu. I love the moody colors of it, but I can't get out there as often as I would like." Someone suddenly jostled her from behind with a loud burst of laughter, sloshing champagne from her glass.

"Oh, dear!' Mrs. Henderson cried. "Did you stain your lovely dress?"

"Not at all." Maddie glanced down at her satin skirt and her beaded T-strap heels. "I'm afraid it landed on your beautiful carpet."

Alice frowned as she looked around her drawing

room, which had grown even more crowded in only the few minutes they had been talking. "I don't even know half these people! I did tell my husband I wasn't sure about the whole movie business, but he would insist."

"Is Mr. Henderson very interested in films, then?"

"He thinks they're the coming art form, but I'm not so sure. They always need more and more money, and it all seems to vanish into some kind of black hole. We don't have that much cash, you know? Give me a book or painting any day; those creations are so wonderfully *quiet*. Most of the time." She gave a soft giggle. "Though, I must say that Rex Neville is rather a work of art himself."

Maddie laughed. "I quite agree. I've never seen anyone like him in real life, or like Bridget Bishop."

"I was talking to that rather lovely gentleman over there," Alice said, gesturing toward a man across the room. He was taller than the movie actors, with broader shoulders, his salt-and-pepper hair cropped short, but still very good-looking. "He's a cameraman. He said people with angular, sharply cut features always photograph the best. Apparently, Mr. Bishop is very good at finding such beautiful creatures for his films, but not so good at keeping them. He also told me about such fascinating things as medium focus to make people look younger, and tracking shots to make a set look enormous. I never knew movies were such complicated beasts!"

"It all sounds very artistic. Like setting up a painting,"

Maddie said. She couldn't help but wonder what "good at finding them but not keeping them" meant. Luther Bishop was a famous director. Surely actors *wanted* to work with him?

"Yes. Maybe my husband is right about films, or at least some of them. It sounds like this Mr. Bishop has been making something rather like profitable advertising prints, and now wants to be Rembrandt." Alice took a sip of her pink drink, and suddenly exclaimed, "Who on earth is *that*?"

Maddie glanced over her shoulder to see a woman standing as if posed in the doorway, and she was indeed quite a sight. Short and round, draped in a flowing frock of black silk printed with large, multicolored flowers, with a hat that resembled nothing so much as a pot over-flowing with geraniums and peacock flowers on her frizzed hair. She peered out at the gathering through black-framed spectacles and adjusted the enormous black alligator handbag on her arm.

"I think I saw her on the plaza yesterday," Maddie said. "Surely no two people could have a hat like that."

"I should hope not," Alice murmured.

"Oh, I see the colorful Evie has decided to descend on us," a man's voice said, full of laughter. "What fun."

Maddie turned away from studying the flowerpot hat to see the man who had joined them. He was tall and lean, boyishly handsome in a "Tennis, anyone?" way, with a thin mustache and a very flashy orchid-colored suit. She immediately liked the twinkle in his dark-blue eyes, the smile that curved his lips.

"You know her?" Alice said.

"Oh, yes. Evelyn DuLaps. She has a gossip column in *Silver Screen* magazine, very popular. She delights in skewering everyone, especially in popping the very biggest egos. We're all terrified of her. You never want to see one of those hats bobbing your way."

"What is she doing all the way out here in Santa Fe, then?" Maddie asked.

"She must smell a juicy story," the man said. "She can, you know, even one hundreds of miles away, when the wind is right. I wonder who she has in her sights?"

"I think I saw her in town yesterday," Maddie said. "She did seem rather on the track, like a bloodhound, but I didn't see any famous foxes nearby."

"Ha!" the man cried. "That's a good one. But I fear she can trace them even when they go to ground. No hiding from Evie. I'm Phil Ballard, by the way."

"Oh, how rude of me not to make introductions! I'm afraid I was quite stunned by that chapeau," Alice said. "Mr. Ballard, this is Mrs. Madeline Alwin, one of our wonderful Santa Fe artists. Madeline, Mr. Ballard is one of the actors on this shoot."

"Second lead in this cursed flick, I'm afraid, and the villain," Phil Ballard said, shaking Maddie's hand.

"Why cursed?" she asked.

"Oh, accidents with the cameras, people leaving, gossipmongers like Evie DuLaps lurking around while everyone cowers in their boots. The usual movie stuff, I suppose."

"How interesting," Maddie said. "I never realized how dangerous the business really was! Surely it will liven things up here in our quiet town."

"Not usually very fascinating, I'm sorry to say," Phil laughed. "It's almost always dull as watching paint dry, all waiting around for hours to make one shot, costume fittings, stuff like that. I'd rather be an artist, like you, and live out here in this wondrous open air. Even if it *is* quiet."

"Not always so quiet, I'm afraid," Alice said. "There was a murder just a few months ago. Madeline here was right in the middle of it all!"

"Really?" Phil's eyes widened as he studied Maddie. "You must tell me all about it. I am a great lover of all things detective novel."

"I am, too," Maddie said. "Especially Chesterton books! But the murder here wasn't so interesting." And it had indeed touched her own house, taking away Juanita's husband—even if he wasn't that much of a husband. She didn't like to think about it all.

"I still want to hear about it." Phil took a sip of his

wine and glanced around. "And who is *that*? You don't happen to know him, do you? Such a dashing cravat!"

Maddie looked to where he was gesturing and saw it was Gunther, who was waving his cigarette and laughing merrily at something one of the waiters was saying. The green-and-white polka-dotted cravat she had brought him from New York gleamed. *Hmm*, she thought, glancing thoughtfully between Phil Ballard and her friend. Could it possibly be? Poor Gunther had been without a romance in so long, and was so lonely. "Oh, yes. He's my neighbor and wonderful friend, Mr. Gunther Ryder. He's a writer, and quite one of my favorite people."

Phil smoothed his hair and twitched at his blue-and-gold-striped necktie. It was almost as splendid as Gunther's own neckwear. "Perhaps you could introduce me? I do so love—literature."

"In front of your gossip columnist?" Maddie whispered.

Phil waved his hand. "She's not interested in small fry like me, my dear. She's after much bigger fish, see?"

Maddie saw that Evelyn DuLaps had indeed latched on to Rex Neville. She stood at his elbow, whispering to him intently as he stared at her in obvious bewilderment.

"Then I'll be happy to introduce you," Maddie said, but then she thought of Gunther's last two heartbreaks, when a man he thought he was falling in love with abruptly decamped to California, and an aspiring writer he befriended turned out to be a thug. "But I warn you, he *is* a very dear friend of mine, and I never like to see my friends get hurt."

"You have my word of honor, dear lady," he said solemnly. "I am no cad. Just a well-brought up lad of the prairies, honest and true."

Maddie laughed. "I can see that." But she had barely taken his arm to lead him through the crowd when the back door leading to the garden opened, and a couple appeared. The man was older and what was usually called "distinguished looking," with iron-gray hair, thick and shining, brushed back in a pompadour, and a mustache framing his sensual lips and strong jaw. The lady on his arm, though, looked barely old enough to be called a lady and not just a girl. She was very small, flapper-slim in an unfashionable white organdy dress, her glossy black hair twisted atop her head and escaping in untidy tendrils from its pins. She swayed on her pink satin shoes, looking so pale her dark eyes burned like coals against the milky whiteness. She looked around as if bewildered to find herself there, and the crowd grew quiet.

"Who is that?" Maddie whispered to Phil.

"Don't you know? That's our illustrious director himself, Luther Bishop. I don't know the girl, though."

Maddie thought she might. But the last time she'd seen her, the girl hadn't looked as if she was about to faint. She had been smiling and bubbly as she sold Maddie and Juanita a bag of lemons. "That's the daughter of Mr. Ortiz, who owns a small fruit store near the plaza. Her name is Maria. She's quite the local belle; she was Reina of the Fiesta last year. The big season of balls and parades that mark the Spanish return to Santa Fe in the 1600s. They always choose a queen." Maddie looked at Maria's hand clutching at the white sleeve of Mr. Bishop's dinner jacket. Maria looked up at him with dilated eyes and smiled. "She's barely sixteen, though!"

Phil's lips twisted in a disgusted frown. "Oh, that won't stop our Luther, you know."

"Bridget, my dear," Luther said, loud enough for everyone to hear. "I think I've found the perfect beauty to play your daughter in our little film. This is Maria Ortiz. Isn't she a pretty one? A star in the making, I would say."

Maddie glanced at Bridget Bishop, whose beautiful, ivory heart of a face seemed frozen into the image of a marble Grecian goddess statue, perfectly still, her thoughts tucked firmly away behind her large green eyes. A tiny smile quirked at the corner of her bow lips, perfectly painted rosy pink, as she looked steadily back at her smirking husband.

Everyone around Maddie seemed to be trying to pretend they were focused on their own cocktails, their own cigarettes and conversation, but really they were just watching the Bishops. A sort of breathless anticipation hung in the air, as if everyone was caught up in a movie scene. Indeed, the whole tableau had a strong whiff of "scene" about it all, something rehearsed and perfected many times before. It made Maddie feel fidgety and uncomfortable to watch, as she had grown up in a world where a person's relationships were a private thing. Her mother hated *scenes* above all else.

But Maddie had to admit there was a terrible fascination to it all. The Bishops, after all, were professionals.

Bridget Bishop took a long drag on her cigarette in its ivory holder. "A star in the making, is it, darling?" she said, a touch of an Irish brogue in her silvery voice. "Well, perhaps before you rush her to makeup, you should find the poor, wee thing a basin. She looks as if she'll be sick at any moment."

Miss Ortiz was indeed looking rather green. She swayed dangerously, her eyes fluttering closed. Luther Bishop caught her as she nearly toppled over, and Alice Henderson leaped forward with a faience bowl just as the girl lost her champagne. Alice took her arm and gently led her out of the room, and Luther turned away with a disgusted twist to his lips.

Bridget looked down at her cigarette with a half grimace, half smirk. "The young ones are always overwhelmed—at first. They soon get over it, though, don't they, darling?" she called after her husband. "You make sure of *that*."

Everyone suddenly rushed back into the whoosh of conversation, eager to pretend nothing had happened. Luther Bishop vanished into the crowd, and Bridget turned away to let Rex Neville light another cigarette for her. Maddie suddenly felt cold and queasy, and she knew she had to find Gwen.

"Excuse me for a moment, Mr. Ballard," she murmured to Phil, who nodded. She gave her half-empty glass to one of the maids and searched through the crowd, which had grown even thicker. The smell of smoke and expensive perfume was heavy in the air, the sound of laughter louder and more frantic. A few couples rolled up the gray-and-white Navajo rugs and turned up the music to launch into an energetic foxtrot. Maddie went up on tiptoe to try to see past all the sparkle of beaded dresses and the sheen of brilliantined hair.

Finally, she found Gwen tucked into a slightly quieter curtained window embrasure with Will and Lorelei. They had procured what looked like a bottle of the local moonshine, Pojoaque Lightning, and were laughing together as they lolled on the red and turquoise-blue cushions of the adobe window seat. Gwen looked relaxed and happy, and Maddie hoped maybe she hadn't seen the little Bishop tantrum, and poor Maria Ortiz getting sick.

But when she sat down beside Gwen, she saw that her cousin's eyes were a little too bright, a slash of red flush on her powdered cheeks. Maddie took the half-full glass from Gwen's hand and dared a sip. Yes—Lightning. It burned as it went down.

"Oh, Mads, I was just telling Lorelei about all the high jinks William here got up to in his misspent Manhattan youth," Gwen said with a high, sharp laugh. "All those silly pranks!"

"I'll find that most of them were your idea, Gwen dear," Maddie said lightly, as she surreptitiously tipped the Lightning into a potted palm.

"Was it?" Gwen said. "Yeah, maybe so."

Lorelei laughed, and nudged Will's shoulder as he blushed adorably. "Well, it all sounds like stuff Will would do. He's always playing jokes on the set. Keeps things lively. I don't know what we would do without him."

Maddie smiled at her. Lorelei really was very pretty, with her red-gold hair and dark eyes, and of course very well dressed, as befitted a wardrobe designer. The cream and gold layers floated like a cloud around her, the colors cleverly layered to give it a subtle shimmer. Maddie could definitely envision her onscreen. "Will says you also act, as well as design fashions. I envy you having so many talents."

Lorelei smiled. "Just wardrobe for now, I'm afraid. I

sure wouldn't mind acting, though. I do get awfully bored sometimes."

"And she has to put up with temperamental sorts fussing about their clothes," Will said. "They're never happy. I would end up decking some of them, but Lorelei here is as patient as a peach."

"Oh?" Maddie said. "Are there lots of tantrums backstage?"

Lorelei laughed. "Most of them are absolute ducks, really. And I've found that the more famous they are, the nicer they are. I dressed Lillian Gish once for her last flick, and she couldn't have been sweeter. But a few can be right cows, as my Cockney grandma used to say. I charge them extra."

"Like right now," Will said.

"It's true the Bishops pay well on their projects," Lorelei said. "No one would work with them otherwise, famous or not. Just remember, Will darling—this film will be a big leg up for us."

Maddie remembered what Will had said, that he hoped this project would bring him more work, and that he planned to write a corker of a script for Lorelei when it did. "I would guess a big costume flick could be fun. Hoopskirts and bonnets and such."

"I did a French Revolution thing last year," Lorelei said. "Now *that* was fun. Marie Antoinette and everything, lots of satin and feathers. Luther Bishop insists he wants 'authenticity' on this one, lots of drab old calico and sun-bonnets. And poor Gwennie here gets it the worst, being the maid and everything."

Gwen, who had been worryingly quiet up till then, gave a little, sad smile. "It's not so bad, now that you per-suaded Luther I could just wear that black dress with the white collar. It's sort of Chanel-like, right?"

"Sure," said Lorelei, patting her arm. "You look chic in anything! And Rex Neville looks nice in chaps and cowboy boots, too, and we can find him a lovely big hat with a beaded band. I have to say, my assistant girls think he's a bright spot in our dull days of fittings!"

"Hey, now!" Will said in mock outrage. "I'm sure I could look nice in a cowboy hat and some flashy boots, too."

"I'll have to take you shopping soon, then," Maddie said with a laugh. Gwen sagged against her shoulder, sud-denly heavy, as if the tiredness had caught up with her, and Maddie wrapped her arm around her cousin. "For now, though, I should probably get Gwen home. She's surely tired after her long trip out here to Santa Fe."

"I'm not," Gwen protested weakly. "But I wouldn't mind going back to your house for some of your Juanita's excellent cocoa."

Will stood up and held out his hand to help Gwen. "I'll drive you back, then, and come back for Lorelei."

"Oh, no, I'll come with you," Lorelei said, draining the last of her drink. "The Hendersons are awfully nice, but I've had enough of that boring Bishop show for the night."

As they left their window hidey-hole, they nearly bumped into Bridget Bishop herself, who was stalking across the room with a frown on her face. She quickly erased it and hid behind a brilliant smile.

"Oh, Lorelei," she said. "There you are. I need to talk to you about my costume for the church social scene. It's entirely unsatisfactory, I'm afraid."

Lorelei gave her a patient nod. "I'm afraid we were just leaving, Mrs. Bishop. We can meet on the set first thing tomorrow. I'm sure we can fix whatever is wrong with the costume."

Bridget sighed, and lit another cigarette in her ivory holder. Her gaze barely flickered over the drooping Gwen before she dismissed her with a twist of her lips. "Oh, very well. Tomorrow, then." Her attention drifted to Maddie, who had to resist the urge to stand up straight and smooth her gown, as if her old nanny were inspecting her. Bridget's sharp green eyes did seem to catch everything. "I don't think we've met."

"Madeline Vaughn-Alwin," Maddie said. "How do you do."

"Oh, yes. The Astor who came out here to paint things. Fascinating," Bridget said, in a faint tone that suggested there was nothing fascinating about it. That, in fact, it all sounded quite mad. "Oh, don't look so surprised, my dear; it's my job to know everything about people. Study them, learn their stories. Just like that dreadful DuLaps woman, I suppose. I saw her lurking around this party. Why she would come all this way to the back of beyond, I have no idea."

"I told Maddie she should try her hand at some art direction," Will said.

Bridget gave her another long, appraising look, which made Maddie want to squirm. "We always need talented artists. Audiences these days expect movies to look so wonderfully grand. Do come by the set, Mrs.—Alwin, was it? We can see if we might suit. Maybe tomorrow?"

Maddie's curiosity had always been stronger than her discomfort, and she admitted she was aching to know what a *real* movie set was like. "I'd like that, thank you, Mrs. Bishop."

"Oh, call me Bridget, please. I do rue the day I took on the name Bishop." She glanced again at Gwen, a look of mingled exasperation and pity. "And Gwendolyn, dear, do try and pull yourself together. You have a scene to film tomorrow, and no one has time for multiple takes again. You weren't the first, you know, and you won't be the last." She sighed and turned to drift away on a wave of lamé and Shalimar.

"What a witch," Gwen muttered at her back. Maddie

glanced down at her to see that Gwen's face was flushed again, and she swayed a bit on her silver high heels.

"We should get home," Maddie said. "This party has rather lost its luster, I think. But first, let's find young Miss Ortiz. We can drop her off at her parents' shop, the poor kid."

★　★　★

After Maddie had tucked Gwen up in bed with a cup of cocoa and a sleeping powder, and then made sure she was really asleep, she found that she herself didn't feel tired at all. She changed her evening dress for pajamas and a fluffy dressing gown and went to the kitchen to see if there was any cocoa left.

Juanita wasn't asleep yet, either. She sat at the table with a stack of movie mags, Buttercup snoring at her feet and the kettle boiling.

"How was the party, Señora Maddie?" she asked curiously.

Maddie poured out a mug of steaming water and reached for the tin of Monarch Cocoa. "Very interesting."

"Were there lots of stars there?"

"A few. Bridget Bishop, and Rex Neville, and Phil Ballard. They were all very good-looking." She didn't want to tell what had really happened yet—the Bishops' argument, the Ortiz girl, the gossip columnist wandering around digging dirt. She had to process it all herself first, and she didn't want to entirely disillusion Juanita with the lack of true glamour. The fact that it all seemed rather sordid. She sat down across from Juanita and reached for one of the copies of *Photoplay*. A portrait of Bridget Bishop was on the cover. She was all ivory and gold in a white fur coat, a mysterious half smile on her carmine-red lips.

"Was it all very grand?" Juanita said.

"I don't think I would want to hang about with movie stars all the time, let's put it that way," Maddie said, flicking through the glossy pages. "But the clothes were heavenly. I'll have to do some sketches to show the twins. What do these articles say about the Bishops and their work?"

Juanita shrugged. "Bridget Bishop likes to bake shortbread, or so *Silver Screen* says. It reminds her of her childhood in an ancient Irish castle. I don't know anyone who would do their baking in a black lace dress, though, like she does in the photo."

Maddie laughed, remembering Bridget's silver gown at the party, her perfectly coiffed hair and bright slick of immaculately applied lipstick. "I doubt Mrs. Bishop has ever even seen an oven, in Ireland or otherwise."

"The recipe sound good, though, even if it's not really hers. I might give it a try." Juanita showed her a page from the magazine, a picture of Bridget Bishop posed with a bowl and wooden spoon in that black lace gown, and a sidebar with the complicated shortbread recipe, along with one for orange marmalade. "And this says the Bishops were childhood sweethearts, cruelly separated by their families until they found each other again. They've been married for years—no children, though. That's sad."

"Indeed," Maddie murmured, thinking of poor Gwen and Miss Ortiz, and who knew how many others. Bridget Bishop had certainly put up with a lot in her years of marriage.

"It also says they're one of the happiest couples in Hollywood."

"I am not sure I entirely believe that." Maddie found a page that featured "the movie's newest heartthrob matinee idol, Rex Neville." The face that had been heart-stoppingly handsome in real life was beyond beautiful in the photo, his head turned almost in profile to reveal the sweep of his dark hair, the straight, elegant angles of his nose and cheekbones. Maddie scanned the article, which she saw was by none other than Evelyn DuLaps. *Movie Talk With Aunt Evie.*

"I met him tonight, too," she said.

Juanita gasped as she looked at the photo. "My goodness. Can men *really* look like that?"

Maddie laughed. "This one does." She quickly scanned the column. It seemed Rex had been born on a real ranch in Wyoming but had gone East to be educated at the finest schools and had been discovered in an amateur production of Shakespeare. He had gained fame in a long string of romantic dramas with women like Swanson and

Norma Talmadge, always dancing the tango and gazing longingly up at balconies. "This says he hopes his next film will be with Fritz Zimmerman in Germany and will show off his true acting skills. It seems Zimmerman wasn't sure about him, but Rex is sure he can prove himself if given the chance."

"I remember this Zimmerman. He directed that movie we saw last year, didn't he? The one with the haunted house that wasn't really a haunted house but a crumbling imperial kingdom, all those strange angles and shadows. Scared the twins to pieces."

"*The Concealing Cabinet*, yes. It was certainly interesting, though I'm not sure I entirely understood it."

"It reminded me of the Masau'u stories from when I was a girl."

"Zimmerman is quite avant-garde, and he's very picky about his actors. I wonder why Rex Neville is here doing a cowboy flick, then, instead of in Germany?"

"Maybe he has to do this movie first? Don't actors have contracts and things like that?"

"Yes." Maddie wondered if Rex Neville was sorry he was out here in the middle of the desert and not stretching his acting wings in Germany. And what about the actor he had replaced, Harry Kelly? What was he doing? "I've been invited to the movie set, Juanita. Why don't you come with me, take a look for yourself?"

There was no time to think about the intricacies of

movie casting, though. The back door opened on a gust of chilly wind, and Juanita's son Eddie stood there with his knapsack.

"Hi, Ma, Señora Maddie," he said with a grin. He had been gone only a few weeks, but Maddie was sure he looked taller, less gangly, more like a young man than a child now. His black hair was longer, his skin tanned from working outside. He looked happier, brighter, than he had since his father died so horribly. "Sorry to get back so late. I should have known you two would be up gossiping about the movies."

Buttercup leaped up to give him doggy kisses, her tail wagging madly, and he laughed and caught her in his arms.

"Eddie!" Juanita cried. She jumped up to give him such a hard, long hug he started squirming. "What on earth are you doing here?"

"I caught a ride home on the dairy wagon from San Ildefonso when they made their delivery," he said. "Kind of last minute, so I didn't have time to phone. I'm starved, though. Anything left from dinner?"

Juanita hurried to take the leftover chicken stew from the icebox, while Maddie made him sit down so she could pour him some cocoa. "I thought you were going to stay with your Uncle Diego through the winter," Juanita said, slicing up some bread.

"I was, but I'm afraid I found out I'm no good at

farming *or* ranching, and he and Uncle Refugio were fed up with me," Eddie said. "So I got a job bussing tables at La Fonda for a while."

Juanita frowned, and plunked a tub of butter down on the table. "If you're not at the pueblo, you should be at school like your sisters."

Eddie made a face. "Maybe next term, yeah, Ma? Right now, I'd rather work, bring in some money." He grinned up at her. "Besides, I hear there are a bunch of movie stars staying at La Fonda. No one would want to miss out on *that*."

CHAPTER 7

The movie set for *The Far Sunset* was several miles outside Santa Fe, near the small village of Valdez, an idyllic setting along a winding river amid a fruit orchard. The mountains rose in the distance, purple and shadowy. It felt very far away from the rest of the world.

The gates at the orchard entrance were shut, guarded by two young boys Maddie wasn't really sure ought to guard so much as a chicken coop, let alone a movie set with film stars and thousands of dollars' worth of equipment. But she supposed Santa Fe wasn't chock-full of burly security guards. Most of *them* were surely working at rum-running, and Inspector Sadler's men weren't a tremendous help. She shuddered a bit to remember her encounters with Sadler during Tomas Anaya's murder case.

One of the boys, who swaggered importantly toward the car as they rolled to a stop, she recognized as Eddie's friend Harry. She could never forget those unruly blond curls. She hoped he wasn't getting into trouble as he had been the last time she'd seen him.

"Harry," she said. "I see you have some new gainful employment. Good for you."

He blushed a bit under his freckles and kicked at the dust. "Hey, it's you, Mrs. Alwin. Didn't think I would run into you again."

"It's a small town." Maddie studied the gates, sturdy, new wrought iron set into old railings. A person couldn't just crash through them. Another expense of Bishop's that the movie backers didn't want to pay? "Does Luther Bishop pay your salary?"

"His studio, I think. That's what on the checks, when he doesn't just give us cash for patrolling. It's a good enough wage."

"Keeps you out of bootlegging trouble, I hope," Maddie said. "Do you have to check passes, that sort of thing?"

"Just keeping the lookie-loos out, Mrs. Alwin," he said, giving her as stern a look as he could, which wasn't very. "I'm sure you understand how it is."

"Of course I do! See you later, Harry," she said, waving as they drove on.

Maddie stepped down from Will's car, Juanita right behind her, and studied the scene in fascination. A large clearing by the river, with the cliffs soaring dramatically behind it, was set up with a covered wagon, a crumbling "adobe" wall that a team of workmen swarmed around, and a large firepit currently unlit.

None of the actors were in sight, not even Gwen, who had left at dawn for an early call. Maddie imagined they must be in hiding in the prefab bungalows in the distance, a line of incongruent white siding and pitched roofs against the tan, olive green, and pale pink of the earth. But the place was still full of people.

She slipped on her tinted glasses so she could see clearly past the sun's glare on the pale cliffs. It was a gorgeous day, the sky an endless stretch of cloudless blue cut into by the hills. The light as usual was piercing, dazzling. Perfect for painting, but she wondered how it would look on film.

"This way, ladies," Will said cheerfully, and led them down the stony pathway to the clearing. Maddie was glad she had worn sturdy flat oxfords and a plain blue tweed suit, even though she had been tempted to put on something more glamorous for a movie set. But it seemed the films weren't quite as elegant in the making as in the seeing.

She glimpsed a long table under a tent, lined with sandwiches, cakes, and enormous urns of tea and coffee, where extras in long calico gowns and cowboy denims and leather vests lined up. A small, birdlike woman with a measuring tape and scissors ran around taking up sleeves, and a few more workmen brushed past with tools and mysterious mechanical contraptions.

Maddie saw a large camera set up on what looked like a miniature railway track at the edge of the clearing. Bill Ackerman, the cameraman she had met at the Hendersons' party, peered into the viewfinder. Luther Bishop stood at his elbow, yelling something indistinguishable as he waved his arms. He took off his wide-brimmed straw hat and waved that, too, as Bill scowled. Bishop wore a finely tailored suit that seemed strange on the dusty set.

"What do you mean, you can't fix it?" Maddie heard Luther demand as she walked closer. "You're supposed to be the best in the business! I'm paying you a pretty penny to fix things!"

Bill drew back from the camera and stared down at Bishop from his greater, hulking height. Maddie imagined he must be a great deal stronger than the director, but his expression was stoic rather than angry. "Doesn't matter how much you pay, it's like trying to pay to get another day of life. No one can move the sun. Those shadows on the cliff aren't going anywhere anytime soon. You can wait to film the scene till evening, but then you'll lose the light. Location filming's not always a pip, is it?"

Bishop threw up his hands. "Then we'll just have to try something else, won't we? Time is money! Every day we sit here is throwing away another grand. Get out the fog machines!"

"Fog?" Bill said doubtfully.

"We can mask those shadows. Give it all a bit of atmosphere."

Bill shrugged. "Whatever you say. You're the boss."

"And none of you should forget it," Bishop growled. "I sign the checks. What I say goes." He flagged down two men hurrying past, carrying a ladder. "You two! Find the fog machine. Now."

As Luther hurried off, Maddie glanced back at Juanita. Juanita was watching the little scene with a disapproving moue. She hated rudeness.

"Slow start today, Bill?" William asked the cameraman.

Bill rolled a cigarette from a little box he pulled from his pocket and took his time lighting it. "Every day it's a slow start. Takes time to get it all set up. But I ain't seen anyone as changeable as this guy, and I've worked with everyone in the business. It'll be Christmas before this picture even gets close to a wrap."

Will frowned. "No one can afford that."

"Especially not His Majesty Luther Bishop," Bill scoffed.

"What do you mean?" Maddie asked, curious. The film business seemed a strange one, and fascinatingly full of odd characters. "This picture has a big budget, right?"

"Oh, hey, it's Mrs. Alwin, right? From the party?" Bill said, turning to her with a smile. "You all sure know how to keep the fun going here. No booze raids at all. Yeah, the budget is big. The studio needs a prestige project, something to make all those jazz-baby flicks and five-reel slapstick bits look artistic. But no one has bottomless pockets, and Bishop over there has a reputation that's going downhill fast. If he keeps this up, no one will want to work with him, no matter how artistic he is. And he's good at being artistic, one of the best, I'll say that for him." He squinted into a cloud of smoke. "Oh, well. As long as I get paid, I'll stay here. Pretty place."

He pulled a battered paperback out of his back pocket and settled on a tall, high-backed stool as if content to wait however long it took, racking up the books and ciggies. Maddie admired his patience.

Will led Maddie and Juanita toward the row of bungalows. They passed costume assistants rushing past carrying old-fashioned bonnets, script girls with piles of papers, and people who seemed to be hurrying as fast as they could for no discernible purpose.

Juanita studied the bustle from under the brim of her plain black hat. "If they're having money troubles, Mr. Royle, why don't they just film back in California? I've heard there's pretty scenery there, as well as large warehouses for sets. It must cost a great deal to pay for all these people to come out here and hang about. And doesn't Señor Murphy own this orchard? Everyone knows he's an old penny pincher. How wouldn't rent his place cheap, I suspect."

"You're very right, Mrs. Anaya," Will answered wryly. "It's not cheap. But they wanted an authentic look to the picture." He gestured to the silvery ribbon of the river, sparkling under the sun, the sweep of the dramatic cliffs, the purplish mountains in the distance. "It's meant to be a big saga. It's pretty in California for sure, but nothing as beautiful as this. This is special."

Maddie couldn't agree more, but Juanita studied the scene with the same doubtful purse to her lips. She had grown up in New Mexico, had never lived anywhere else. Maddie knew Juanita loved her home, but she didn't see that it was unique. Maddie could see that the deep specialness of the place would potentially give a movie that touch of real magic, that feeling of being in a whole different world, that could raise it above the others and possibly bring real acclaim. But only if someone had—how was it that Bill Ackerman had put it?—bottomless pockets, in order to make it all happen.

Juanita gestured to the crowds of workmen swarming like bees around the base of the cliffs, wheeling a large, fanlike fog machine into place. A blast of heavy, grayish mist burst out, but it only clung to the rocks along the lower slopes and blew off across the waters of the river, not hiding any shadows at all.

"Don't they know they shouldn't interfere with nature that way?" Juanita said. "It looks silly. And my grandmother would have said that the spirits, who tasked us with living in harmony with all beings, would have their revenge if the mountains and waters are damaged. It's dangerous."

"Quite right," a low, husky voice said. Maddie turned to see Bridget Bishop sauntering toward them. Her blonde, bobbed hair was hidden by a wig in a light-brown, Gibson Girl style. A voluminous white flannel dressing gown was draped from her slender shoulders, giving glimpses of a dark-green calico full-skirted gown and white apron beneath. But the "pioneer mother" veneer was broken when she lifted a cigarette in a tortoiseshell holder to her lips.

"My husband is ruining a perfectly lovely scene and making it all look quite ridiculous—as usual," Bridget said. "And now we'll all have to sit around all day, itching in these hideous costumes. While the spirits watch us in scorn. You are so perceptive." Rather than sounding doubtful about the spirits, she shivered and crossed herself. "Are you here to be an extra today, Mrs. . . . ?"

"Mrs. Anaya," Juanita gasped, staring wide-eyed at the movie star. "You—you're Bridget Bishop."

Bridget laughed, a deep, rich, rolling sound that made Maddie realize it was a pity movies had no sound. "So I am. And you, Mrs. Anaya, look as if you would be quite splendid in today's scene—if we ever get around to filming it. You should get into costume, though. Luther can cause as many delays as he likes himself, but he does tend to have a tantrum when the rest of us do it."

Juanita still looked too stunned to answer, and Will said, "Mrs. Anaya is here with me, Bridget, not as an extra. She's Mrs. Alwin's housekeeper, and they're my guests on the set."

Bridget glanced at Maddie and smiled. "Oh, yes. I remember you. The Astor. Well, if you aren't here as extras, I can only hope Mrs. Anaya is taking over the catering, since she's a housekeeper. Breakfast this morning was abysmal. Luther will never listen to me when I say if you treat your company right, *they* will treat you right in return. He's such a boor, so penny-pinching in the weirdest ways and spendthrift in others. It's no surprise this production is going keister-over-teakettle."

"Maddie is an artist, and an old friend of mine," Will said. "I thought she could do a bit of work on the sets, since she knows the aesthetics of the area."

Bridget nodded at Maddie. "Tell me, as an artist, what do *you* think of this little scene?" She waved with her cigarette at the clearing, now shrouded in fake fog so the wagon and adobe wall could barely be seen. The smell was acrid.

"It looks like a cheap Halloween haunted house at a Coney Island fun fair," Maddie said honestly. "Maybe if it was really a scene with the bad spirits descending . . ."

Bridget laughed. "Quite right. It's very vulgar. This isn't meant to be a demon bride flick. My husband doesn't have instincts for real art. If you do, Mrs. Alwin, I would warn you to stay away, for your own sake."

The door of one of the bungalows opened, and a small, mousy woman in a blue smock and spectacles that Maddie had seen earlier hemming sleeves peeked out. "Mrs. Bishop! You're needed in makeup right away."

Bridget sighed. "More hurry up and wait. Coming, Perkins! See you all later, Will, Mrs. Alwin. Mrs. Anaya, I do hope we can talk more later. I am fascinated by these spirits."

She swept off into the bungalow, the door slamming behind her, and Will led Maddie and Juanita toward another, larger building.

"It all sounds as if there's not much confidence in Luther's abilities," Maddie said as they hurried past a cluster of more cowboys drinking coffee and arguing about the White Sox.

Will gave one of his crooked, rueful smiles and shrugged. "This is a new sort of film for him, it's true. But he's managed large casts before, and his name should bring some attention to *The Far Sunset*, as should those of Bridget and Rex."

"But if he's antagonized the crew, and gone over budget and behind schedule . . ."

"It's not behind schedule—yet," Will said. He opened the door and ushered them through, into complete chaos.

The room was long and narrow, lined on one wall with lighted mirrors and tall canvas chairs, with a cluster of tables, chairs, and sofas at the far end. Actors and actresses perched in front of the mirrors, while makeup assistants in pink smocks fluttered around them in clouds of powder. The counters were cluttered with pots of rouge, cakes of mascara, eyebrow pencils, uncapped lipsticks, and wigs on stands, and the stuffy air smelled of talcum and greasepaint and coffee. Voices hummed like a swarm of flies.

Phil Ballard sat at the last mirror, a hairdresser fitting him with a gray-streaked wig that made him look years older while another girl powdered his nose. "Mrs. Alwin! Don't forget you said you would introduce me to your dishy neighbor!" he called.

Maddie laughed. "I won't forget. Come by my house for a cocktail when you're not busy."

He grinned, which made the makeup girl scold him. "We're always busy here, dear, hurrying up to do nothing. But I am holding you to your invitation!"

Just past the makeup line, Lorelei was busy pinning up the hem of a woman perched on a stool. As she twisted around to examine her costume, a long, plain black

poplin dress with white collar and cuffs, like that of a prairie French shopgirl, Maddie saw it was Gwen. Her cousin had left before anyone else was up, and Maddie had been very worried about her after the party. But Gwen looked very well, better than she had since arriving in Santa Fe, her eyes bright with interest. Maybe working *would* help her.

"Quit fidgeting, Gwen, or I'll never get this done," Lorelei muttered through the pins clutched in her teeth.

"Can't we make the hem just a teeny, tiny bit shorter?" Gwen said. She glimpsed Maddie and waved. "Oh, hi, Mads! Sorry I ran out so early this morning. Rex offered me a ride, and I needed to go over this scene."

"I hope you ate some breakfast before you left, Señora Gwen," Juanita said severely.

Gwen laughed, her cheeks pink. She really did look so much better, Maddie thought, as if she had decided on a path forward, a positive path. "No time! I'll grab a raisin roll from catering later, though they're not a patch on *your* fabulous cooking, Juanita. Sure to be too stale."

"Will, it's a good thing you got here," Lorelei said, tying off a thread and dropping her pins in a jar. "Luther was going on about this scene needing some major revisions. He was almost ranting, really! I worry about his health. He needs to eat more whole meal for his heart."

Will made a face. "More revisions? Sorry, Mads, duty calls. Will you be all right here on your own for a while?"

"Of course," Maddie answered him. "We'll just take a little peek around and try not to get in the way."

"You can get some coffee and take a seat over there until shooting gets started, whenever that might be. Just don't go around the corner; that's where Mr. Bishop has his office, off-limits for everyone else," Lorelei said, nodding toward the cluster of chairs and sofas in the corner. "I have to get through that pile of mending. Actresses—such klutzes."

"Hey!" Gwen cried indignantly.

"I can help you with that," Juanita said.

Lorelei beamed at her. "Oh, you're an angel! Workbox is just over there. It's just torn hems, mostly. And no, Gwen, it can't be any shorter. That would be completely historically incorrect."

Maddie made her way toward a velvet-upholstered sofa tucked in the corner where she could watch the action in the room without being underfoot. There was a pile of magazines on the table, and she took up a couple of old *Photoplays*, but what was happening around her was more interesting. The makeup techniques, the chatter, the glow of the lights. Juanita sat down beside her with a pile of calico and muslin to work on, and they whispered together over what they had seen on set.

A group of men came into the room from the bright light outside, real natives and not actors from their looks. They were tall, broad-shouldered, olive-skinned, their dark hair glossy, perfect for their costumes of moccasins, buckskin trousers, and blanket wraps, though Maddie was sure the blankets were Navajo rather than from the local pueblos.

"Be ready for you in just a sec!" one of the makeup girls called. They all came to sit down silently across from Maddie and Juanita, a few whispering among themselves, a few reaching for the magazines and cigarettes.

"Juanita Montoya?" one of them said. "Is that really you?"

Juanita glanced over her shoulder and gave a little gasp. To Maddie's surprise, she even blushed a little, her smooth, bronzed cheeks spotted with rose. Efficient, brisk, kind but practical Juanita never seemed flustered. Curious, Maddie turned to see a tall, handsome man staring at Juanita as if thunderstruck, and wonderfully delighted, to see her. And what a man he was! Like everyone else on the movie set, he was ridiculously good-looking, as if from another planet than mere mortals. He was dressed like a Victorian rancher in a frock coat, but his long, dark hair lay over his shoulders in two braids. Lines fanned out from his chocolate-brown eyes, as if he spent a lot of time in the sun or laughing, but it only made him even more handsome.

Juanita patted at the neat twist of dark, silver-touched hair under the edge of her hat. "My heavens. Francisco. Whatever are you doing here? It's been an age."

He grinned, those lines around his eyes deepening. Maddie glanced between him and Juanita, fascinated. "Ten years, I'd say. The deer dances at Christmas, when your brother Refugio just got married."

"So it was," Juanita murmured. "When I was at San Ildefonso last, a few weeks ago, your sister said you hadn't been home in a long time, but she didn't say where you had gone. I thought maybe you were running an orchard off in the mountains, like you always said you wanted."

"I'm the family black sheep now. Went off to work in the fruit fields in California and ended up in the movies. Got a part in this flick. I couldn't believe it when they said we were coming here. I was—well, I guess I was hoping I would run into you. And here you are, right on the set! Are you acting now, too? You should; you're just as pretty as Gloria Swanson. Just like you always were."

Juanita pressed her gloved fingertips to her lips as if to keep from giggling girlishly. Maddie wished she would just let it out. If anyone deserved a little frivolous laughter, it was her friend, after all she had been through with Tomas Anaya.

"I couldn't act," Juanita said. "I would freeze up as soon as anyone pointed that camera contraption at me. I'm here with Mrs. Alwin, my employer, who is going to do a bit of art—what was it, Señora Maddie?"

"Art direction, but I don't think I have anything to add to the set here," Maddie said. She smiled and held out her hand. "Madeline Alwin. Call me Maddie. I'm always so happy to meet a friend of Juanita. You've known each other a long time, Mr. . . . ?"

He smiled in return and shook her hand. Maddie could see what had come over Juanita; she nearly giggled herself. "Francisco Altumara. Frank. Nice to meet you, Mrs. Alwin. I've known Juanita since we were kids at the mission school together. She was the smartest one in our class; no one could keep up with her. She also made the best apple pies, and always brought them to share, as well as helped with our schoolwork. Such a kind heart."

"Well, nothing has changed. I could never do without her," Maddie said, thinking it was definitely nostalgia week, with Francisco and her own old friend William popping up. And Francisco did seem terribly nice as well as handsome. "You should come to dinner, Mr. Altumara, if you have some time off during filming." She wondered if she should just have a party, with all the invites she was giving out.

"That's kind of you, Mrs. Alwin. I'd certainly like that," Francisco said.

Maddie glanced at Juanita, but she didn't look as if she was going to talk much. She had folded her gloved hands on her pile of mending and looked steadily down at them.

"Have you been in very many movies?" Maddie asked him.

"About twenty. Just small parts, though, but this one

is a little bigger. I'm the head of the band of natives who live near the homestead."

"What's it like working here, with someone like Luther Bishop?" Maddie said. "We've only been here on set for a short while, but it's all so fascinating."

Francisco looked around, as if to see who was nearby. "It's been—interesting," he said softly. "I think my old granny might have said someone put an evil spirit over the production."

That was like what Juanita had said, Maddie thought with a shiver. It did feel as if the set was under a strange spell or something.

"Old Mrs. Altumara was always a superstitious yi-yi," Juanita said, but like Maddie, she looked a bit uneasy.

"What's been happening?' Maddie whispered.

"Just arguments, with everyone, lots of time lost, equipment breaking. I've always wanted to work with Mr. Bishop. His pictures make a lot of money, and they say this one will show he's a real artist, too. But now I don't know."

Before Maddie could ask him more, a young boy came running through the crowded room like a whirl-wind, shouting, "Places, everyone! Shooting starts in five minutes!"

"I'd better be going," Francisco said. He smiled at Juanita, whose cheeks turned pink again. "Maybe I'll see you later, though? Talk about the old days?"

"Maybe so," Juanita answered. "It—it's good to see you again, Francisco. You look—well."

His grin widened, and he hurried away, followed by most of the others. The room emptied astonishingly fast. The makeup girls finished powdering cheeks, and Lorelei tugged Gwen's costume into place before draping a flannel dressing gown over her shoulders.

"My goodness, Juanita, I think you've been holding out on me," Maddie whispered. "He is a looker!"

"We were just school friends once, that's all," Juanita answered.

"Still, how exciting you know a movie actor!" Maddie said. She gulped down the last of her coffee and took Juanita's arm to follow everyone outside. One of the assistants found them a couple of folding chairs in the shade, and they settled in to watch it all, her stomach fluttering with excitement.

She studied the scene. Will stood off to one side of the covered wagon, shuffling through a stack of papers as he passed them out to the actors. Bridget Bishop, Gwen, and Rex Neville, in a large white cowboy hat, stood behind the wagon, reading through the scene while Lorelei fluttered around adjusting their costumes. Phil Ballard, Francisco, and a few others waited off to one side of the clearing as if about to make their entrance. Phil waved to Maddie and smiled broadly, ruining the effect of his villainous black suit and gray wig, as well as a swooping fake mustache he had gained since she last saw him at the makeup table.

Bill Ackerman adjusted his camera, peering into the viewfinder, scowling, changing angles. Luther Bishop strode past him to his director's chair nearby.

"Get that pest out of here right now!" he shouted, and pointed to a figure half hidden near the catering tent, someone Maddie hadn't noticed before. Evelyn DuLaps, the gossip columnist, scribbling into a notebook, her face hidden by her large flowerpot hat. "Who let her in, anyway?"

Evelyn glared at him from under that drooping brim. "Freedom of the press, Mr. Bishop! We live in *America*, you know."

"Right now we're in the kingdom of *my* set, and my cast doesn't need your nosy parker butt-ins distracting them. They have enough trouble concentrating as it is," Bishop said. "Scram, before I have to call security again."

Evelyn DuLaps gave a huff, but she marched off in smartish fashion. Luther turned to his actors.

"Okay, so we're going to try this scene again, and today we better get it right," he said. "You're supposed to be professionals, but it's like tiny-town summer stock around here."

"Maybe if we had a director who actually knew how to communicate instead of a ham-fisted hack . . ." Bridget muttered, tilting her chin as Lorelei adjusted her wig.

"Bridget, you and Gwen are afraid Phil over there is coming on your land to fulfill his dire threat to take over your homestead by force, burn you out," Luther said. "*Dire* threat. That means at least try to appear afraid. You're a delicate lady from back East who has to be brave for her family. That means more Lillian Gish, less Mabel Normand taking a pie in the face, understand?"

Bridget just shot him a venomous look, but Maddie thought Gwen looked scared enough for both of them. The sparkle in her eye she'd had earlier was gone, and she was pale.

"Rex, you're the ladies' only protection," Luther said. "And you're secretly in love with Bridget here, though who knows why. You're strong and noble, here to melt the audiences' hearts. I know you can do that."

Rex looked disgusted. "It's all I ever do."

Luther just scowled at them all. "And Phil, for heaven's sake, be frightening! Quit mincing around with that mustache for five minutes. You're the terrifying villain. Now, places, everyone, right now! And, action!"

The cameras whirred into motion, and Maddie felt another little thrill to be watching a real movie happening right in front of her. The actors moved across the "homestead" set, the cliffs shimmering behind them, the trees swaying in the wind, and even though there were no words, she found herself engrossed in the drama. Bridget especially was amazing, full of dignity and fear and courage, her face the very image of stalwart womanhood. Maddie could see no hint of "pie in the face" from her at all. And Phil Ballard, with his merry smile gone, seemed frighteningly menacing.

But it all didn't last long. "Cut!" Luther shouted. "What did I tell you all? This is like amateur hour. And we're losing light." He rushed onto the set as Gwen looked as if she would burst into tears, Bridget crossed her arms and glared at her husband, and Phil tapped his booted foot and smoothed his mustache, the evil menace of only a second before having vanished. Rex studied his fingernails.

"Bridget, I said you were meant to be delicate and brave. Subtle. No one is tying you to the railroad tracks right now," Luther said. "Quit rolling your eyes like a Fulton Market fishwife."

"Maybe if you had the skills to set up proper close shots, we wouldn't have to roll our eyes to convey an emotion," Bridget answered. "Subtlety was never your strong suit, was it, darling?"

"Lorelei!" Luther shouted. "Come here and show Mrs. Bishop what delicacy looks like."

Lorelei, who was adjusting Gwen's white collar, turned around with wide, shocked eyes. "Me?"

"You. You have aspirations to act, don't you? And you're young and pretty enough. Show us what you can do."

Lorelei tucked a strand of hair, loosened from its pins, behind her ears and stepped forward. Even Maddie could see she was shaking with nerves. Lorelei glanced at Will, who nodded at her, and she closed her eyes for an instant. When she opened them, she went through Bridget's scene step by step, one hand to her brow, one flung out as if to protect her home. She *was* good, Maddie thought, but she lacked something of Bridget's subtlety.

"See? Like that," Luther said. "Okay, let's run through the scene one more time without film; then we have to get on with it."

Bill Ackerman fiddled with the camera, doing something with a length of film. Fascinated, Maddie drifted closer to examine the equipment.

"What does the scene look like in there?" she asked.

"Want to take a peek?" Bill said.

"Wouldn't I mess it all up?" Maddie said, nervous but very tempted.

He laughed. "Nah, it's all turned off. Here, just peek through the viewfinder."

She went up on tiptoe and peeked through the lens. The scene looked fascinating like that, narrowed into its own small world, like a movie and not just a set. "Amazing," she whispered.

"You turn it like this," Bill said, showing her the reel. "See how it looks from different angles. How the shadows fall that way."

"Like a painting," she said, taking in the cliffs, the

sky, the people who looked so small against the sweep of nature.

"We'll have to reshoot soon or the light'll be gone, and we'll have to set it all up again tomorrow." Bill sighed impatiently. "We're over the schedule as it is."

Maddie focused on the people at the center of the set. Lorelei was adjusting Bridget's costume while Rex and Gwen tried a bit of stage business. The errand boy who had announced places earlier came running up to Luther Bishop and handed him a stack of mail. Through the round lens, Maddie watched as he impatiently sorted through the letters, tossing them back to the boy.

But Luther froze at one, staring down at it with something like shock on his angry face. He looked up, glaring all around, before he scowled again. He crumpled up the paper and threw it on the ground.

"All right, one more chance," Luther shouted, stalking back to his chair. "Places! Now!"

Maddie gave Bill back his camera and went to her seat to watch the scene. Everything seemed to go to Luther's satisfaction this time, the affable Phil turning rather terrifying, making Bridget's eyes widen with fear, and Rex Neville appeared as the noble protector.

Luther called, "Cut!" and everyone scattered. But Maddie noticed the paper still crumpled in the dust. When no one was looking, she scooped it up, curious.

She smoothed the cheap, lined stationery and scanned the dark block letters. *You better stop this picture or else. You've been warned. Pay up.*

"Jeepers," Maddie whispered. Suddenly chilled, she glanced around, but no one was paying attention. Gwen and Bridget were nearly back to the building, wrapped in their dressing gowns, the men smoking by the river, Luther vanished. Juanita was talking to Francisco under the shade of one of the old trees. Only the errand boy was nearby, tidying up.

"He gets letters a lot," the boy said. "Mr. Bishop. He insists we bring the mail out as soon as it gets here, but he usually just tears it up and throws it down. Mrs. Bridget tells him not to litter, as it's unhygienic."

"Really? All the time?" Maddie read the note again. Surely it had something to do with the budget troubles everyone said the picture was running into, but what? Impulsively, she stuffed it into her handbag. "Well, I would say Mrs. Bridget is quite right."

She glanced up, studying the set. Everyone just seemed to be going about their own business, but something caught her attention, a flutter of something high up on one of the hilly slopes, like a flag tossed by the breeze. Something like a flash of jewelry gleamed, a white robe, a figure. But the light shifted, blinding Maddie for a moment, and when she looked again, it was gone. As if it really was a ghost.

She decided to go in search of Gwen.

The makeup room was empty with everyone on set, echoing, the only light dusty rays of sun floating through the grimy windows. The deserted makeup tables were scattered with a mess of open powder compacts, tubes of lipstick, magazines, overflowing ashtrays, hairpins and nets. A few costumes were tossed over screens, frock coats, cowboy's chaps, a black dress like the one Gwen had worn but without its white lacy collar. A long, dark wig on a stand fluttered suddenly, making Maddie gasp.

"Hello! Is anyone here?" she shouted.

There was always something a little eerie about usually busy places when they were empty. Nightclubs, schools, theaters—movie sets. Wind whirled over the tin roof, and the air was stuffy with the scent of old coffee, powder, greasepaint, and Shalimar perfume. So many ladies wore it, including Lorelei Fontaine and Bridget Bishop, and its heavy, Oriental floral scent did tend to stick. Maddie knew it was hopelessly fuddy-duddy of her, but she preferred her lilac water.

Maddie hurried toward the rooms at the back, the ones used as offices, and noticed a table near a closed door holding a gold-rimmed ashtray with a couple of roughly hand-rolled cigarette butts, and two glasses with the dregs of some amber liquid, one of them stained with rosy-red lipstick smears. A torn bit of paper was half singed in the ashtray.

"Is anyone there?" she asked again, and listened closely. She heard a strange creaking noise and pushed open the office door.

"Oh, no. No, no, no," she gasped, but she feared this was a sight that couldn't be stopped. That she was not likely to forget anytime soon.

A man was hanging from the rafters, stiff and silent, quite dead, swinging with a horrible, slow gentleness. He wore a fine suit, she noticed inanely, pale-gray wool. A metal stool was on its side near the door, as if kicked away, and the warm, humid air smelled horribly of death, as well as an under-tinge of that perfume and of good whiskey.

Maddie pressed her fingers hard to her mouth and forced herself to look at his face. Blue and swollen, his eyes bulging. A tie, blue-and-gold striped, was tied around his neck, and drool or something even worse had left a dried trail on his shaved cheek.

Luther Bishop. And he was quite, quite dead.

CHAPTER 8

"Who would want to kill Luther Bishop?" Inspector Sadler said, pacing the length of the makeup room as he glared at the gathered group from under his bushy eyebrows. He kept taking off and slapping back on his usual bowler hat. "Or why would he want to kill himself? Something shady is going on here."

Maddie sighed. Surely it would be easier to ask, "Who *didn't* want to kill Luther Bishop?" She'd known him for only a day, and she quite loathed him. He was obnoxious, insulting, a harasser of women. She wasn't sure she had met anyone who liked him at all, and that certainly included his wife.

But from what she had seen, it hadn't been murder. It looked like Bishop had hanged himself. Maybe the money troubles she had heard hinted of had gotten to him. Not that he had seemed the type to doubt himself at all.

Bridget Bishop gave Maddie a sympathetic smile and handed her a cigarette. Ever since Inspector Sadler's arrival with his officers after Will phoned the police station, Bridget had been sitting beside Gwen, smoking ciggie after ciggie in her tortoiseshell holder, wrapped in her white dressing gown. The chaos and bustle of the set had gone ominously quiet.

"Let the taste of the smoke linger in the back of your throat, Mrs. Alwin," Bridget said. "It takes that sticky stench of death away."

Maddie didn't usually smoke, but today she took a grateful drag.

Bridget patted her hand. "You get used to it."

Maddie remembered finding Tomas Anaya's body behind La Fonda, and now here was another gruesome discovery. She wasn't sure she would ever get used to such things. She'd make a terrible cop. Or doctor. She took another deep intake of cherry-tinged smoke and glanced around the room at everyone else gathered there. Gwen sat near them on a tall stool, sniffling into a handkerchief, her eyes red-rimmed. Rex Neville was reading a book, a battered old copy of Goethe, though he had put it down to watch the inspector, as calm as if he were observing a play at the Lyceum. Lorelei and Will whispered together, while Bill and the other cameramen stood near the window, Bill with his arms crossed and toes tapping impatiently. Phil

Ballard wasn't there yet. Two of the inspector's men guarded the door.

"Are *you* used to it, Mrs. Bishop?" Maddie asked her. She studied Bridget's beautiful face, which looked quite serene, faraway and ethereal. Unlike Gwen, her eyes were dry.

Bridget gave a harsh little laugh. "My grandparents ran a funeral home when they got here from Ireland. Tiny town in upstate New York; everyone came to them. After my mam died and I went to live with them, I helped with wakes and such. Till they died, too, and I went to the convent." She lit a fresh ciggie. "Preferred the funeral home to the nuns."

That was not at all what *Photoplay* had said her background was, Maddie noted. Irish castles and such.

"Mrs. Bishop," Inspector Sadler said, coming to a stop in front of the new widow. Maddie hadn't seen much of him since Tomas Anaya's killer was caught, but Sadler hadn't changed. He was still portly in his old tweed suit, red-faced, bulldoggish in his questions. "Perhaps I could interview you first, in the small office next to your husband's?"

"Of course," Bridget said with a gracious smile. "Though I don't think I have much to tell you. I haven't seen Luther for hours, not since the last scene wrapped. We didn't speak unless we had to." She rose from her chair and smoothed her white dressing gown. She handed Maddie the pack of cigarettes. Chesterfield, she noticed, unusual for a lady. Some of the butts in the ashtray outside Luther's office had been Chesterfields, but there had also been dark Gauloises and a couple that looked hand rolled, like the ones Bill Ackerman made.

"Take as many as you like, Mrs. Vaughn-Alwin, and share them around if anyone needs some." Bridget glanced at the sobbing, disheveled Gwen, and sighed. "Poor Gwendolyn looks as if she could use one. Or a dozen."

As Bridget followed the inspector from the room, Maddie went to sit next to Gwen. She laid her hand gently on her distraught cousin's arm. "Are you going to be all right?"

Gwen yanked away, covering her eyes with the hankie. "I'm fine. It's all just so silly! Why on earth would Luther chill himself off like that? He had everything he wanted. Men always seem happy when they get what they want, and they *always* do. And why is that cop being so obnoxious? Doesn't he have anything better to work on than harass us?"

Maddie sighed. She knew very well from past experience that Inspector Sadler wasn't the most fun person to be around. After Tomas Anaya was killed and Sadler was sure Eddie had done it, he had annoyed her household to no end. Most of the crime in Santa Fe seemed to be related to alcohol or bad driving, and Sadler was determined to be well known for his dedication to "law and order." So the chance of a case involving famous movie people on his watch made him pounce like an overweight cat.

But she couldn't help but wonder if Gwen was right. Why *would* Luther off himself, right at the start of making a big, prestigious picture? He didn't seem like the depressive, self-doubting type.

Maddie closed her eyes and made herself remember the scene of Bishop's body, as repugnant as it was. *Pretend it's a film scene*, she told herself, *or a scene in a Chesterton mystery.* She remembered the table with the glasses and ashtray, the smear of lipstick, rosy pink. A desk near the body, piled with untidy stacks of papers, a metal strongbox, a gold watch and enameled cufflinks in a small dish.

It surely wasn't a robbery, then, and the set seemed fairly secure with the guards and gates, even if it was a very busy place. Maddie supposed someone *could* sneak down from the top of the mesa, but it would be quite a trip on foot to the bungalows and back.

She remembered the rest of the room, surprisingly small for a director's office. A wardrobe door a bit ajar, a blue-and-red Persian rug, the scripts and notes on the desk, the framed photo of Bridget. No other pictures of girls, an overflowing wastepaper basket, a desk chair. That was about all.

She swallowed hard past a bitter, sick knot in her throat and thought of the body itself, hanging from the light fixture in the middle of the room. The knotted tie around his neck, already slipping a little loose, a blue-and-gold stripe. Where had she seen that before? Maybe Luther himself had worn it, to the Hendersons' party or something. She thought of his shoes, perfectly polished brown wingtips dangling above the toppled stool.

Wait a minute.

Maddie mentally backed up a step and tried to think of what bothered her about that image. Of course, the metal stool. It seemed—backward, somehow, behind the direction of his feet.

Maddie frowned. She wasn't sure what exactly a flailing body might do as it struggled to breathe. It was probably untidy; a footstool could be kicked over and go anywhere. But if he had been standing on it to start . . .

She felt a cold hand on her arm, and she gasped in shock. Her eyes flew open, and she saw Will looking at her in concern.

"Sorry to startle you, Maddie," he said, offering her a glass of water. "You do look awfully pale."

"Thanks," she said, and gulped down the lovely cool liquid. She hadn't realized how dizzy and faint she felt. "I guess it's not every day a girl finds a body."

Will shuddered. "Why would Luther Bishop do such a thing?"

"That's just what I was thinking."

Maddie glanced at Gwen, who had wandered over to stare out the window. She no longer sobbed, but her face was white as a sheet, her eyes puffy and red. "It seems a little far-fetched, I know. It looks so obviously suicide. But there's just something a little—off about the whole thing, isn't there? And Luther Bishop wasn't the most popular person around."

"True enough. He's extravagant with studio money, goes over budget and over schedule, doesn't play nice with actors or writers or anyone, really. Pesters wives and daughters. People put up with him because his pictures make bank, but if someone had had enough . . ."

Maddie studied everyone gathered around, all of them whispering quietly together or else lost in their own thoughts. Lorelei sat sewing, her white cotton dress pale and pristine. Maddie thought of the ghostly figure she thought she had glimpsed at the cliffs. She studied Will carefully. How well did she really know him now? What would his movie ambition lead him to?

But she didn't have time to remember anything else. The office door opened and the body was carried out by two of the inspector's officers. The lumpen shape under a pale sheet made the whole room fall into silence, and Gwen gave a gasping sob that was the only sound. The door was left ajar, and the inspector was still with Bridget in the other office.

"I'll be back in a jiffy," Maddie whispered to Will. "Just have to powder my nose. Can you look after Gwen?"

"Of course," he answered, and went to sit down beside Gwen.

Maddie hurried down the short corridor toward the lavatory behind the offices. She could hear Sadler's voice from behind a closed door, haranguing, and Bridget protesting. Two officers stood outside the door, but they seemed more interested in gossiping together about movie stars than watching suspects and didn't even glance at her when she walked by. The table was still there, with its cigarettes and lipstick-stained glass.

Maddie glanced over at them, then at the half-open door of Luther's office. She peeked in and found it momentarily empty. Impulsively, she ducked inside.

Just by the door was a table with three chairs, apparently a place for conferences and meetings. She glanced over the desk, which was mostly tidy, holding a blotter, a crystal vase filled with pens, a photo of Bridget, and a locked strongbox, just as she remembered. She peeked into the trash can and noticed a few torn letters. Impulsively, she snatched them up and tucked them into her handbag with the other note.

She had barely slid back into her seat when the inspector reappeared with Bridget. The actress's serenity looked a bit shaken, her cheeks reddened, her lips pinched in anger. She stalked out of the bungalow. Sadler ran a gimlet eye over the rest of the crowd, who were suddenly very busy sewing and studying scripts, not meeting his gaze. Next to Maddie, Gwen was trembling. Maddie put her arm around her.

"Miss Astor, I . . ." Sadler's watch suddenly fell on Maddie. "Mrs. Alwin. So nice of you to be here today. Maybe I could have a quick word? If you're not too busy, that is."

Maddie squeezed Gwen's shoulders. Her cousin was sniffling again. Maddie knew all too well how overbearing the man could be. He had just barreled in headfirst on the Tomas Anaya case, a newcomer to town, not knowing anything about Santa Fe and its people, accusing poor Eddie of the crime and refusing to look at any more evidence. She couldn't imagine he had suddenly changed his ways. Definitely better she talk to him before he got to Gwen.

"Are you going to be okay here for a little longer, Gwennie dear?" she whispered, pressing a clean handkerchief into Gwen's trembling hand. "Will can stay with you. I'm sure I won't be gone long."

"I'll be fine," Gwen said, and tried to give her a shaky smile.

"I'll stay with her, too," Lorelei said. "Look, the caterer has brought some sandwiches, the angel. I think we should all try to eat something."

"Just don't go far, any of you," Sadler boomed. "We want to talk to all of you."

Maddie gave Gwen's hand one more squeeze and followed Sadler to the small office next to Luther's. Besides holding desks, telephones, and typewriters for the secretaries, it was obviously used for costume storage. It was lined with racks of linen-covered clothes that fluttered like ghosts in the breeze coming from the small, open window. Stacks of hatboxes and shoe trees were everywhere, crowded around in a scented mélange of different perfumes and colognes, talcum powder, and stale sweat. Maddie was glad of the occasional whiffs of pine-scented air. Her head was whirling after all the horrid sights of the day.

She sat down across from the inspector at one of the desks, which was already piled with notes and stained coffee cups.

"How can I help, Inspector?" she asked, hoping the man wouldn't take too long.

Sadler sat back in his swivel chair, kicking his feet up on the desk. His shoes, unlike Luther's, had seen better days and were scuffed and dusty.

"You do seem to show up everywhere there's trouble in this town, Mrs. Alwin," he said.

"Hardly. I heard you arrested the Hernandez brothers for cockfighting on Lower San Francisco Street last week. I wasn't there, was I?'

Sadler scowled. "But you were mixed up in that Anaya business. Now this. The governor doesn't like big shots from out of state coming here stirring up trouble like this. Makes a brand-new state like New Mexico look uncivilized. Could be gangsters again."

Maddie remembered the bootlegging and drug-smuggling rings from Tomas Anaya's murder. It wasn't too far-fetched to think they had loaned money to Luther, or backed his studio, and now wanted their return. "I don't know. But I would hardly be human if I wasn't curious about the movies. Besides, my cousin is in the cast. She invited me to the set, and that's why I'm here. I've also been asked to do bit of art direction for the scenes. Perfectly understandable."

"Yes. Miss Astor. Always been prone to hysterics, has she? My officers said she's barely stopped crying all day."

"Her director was just found hideously deceased, Inspector. What do you expect?"

Sadler leaned closer across the desk, swinging his feet down again. "We hear he was a bit more than her director."

Maddie felt suddenly cold at the insinuation. She glanced down at the handbag on her lap, where she had stashed the threatening note. "She doesn't tell me much about her personal life, so I can't help you there."

"Mr. Bishop was quite the ladies' man, at least according to his wife, as well as Miss DuLaps. I'm sure once we question the others, they'll say the same."

"Miss DuLaps? The gossip columnist?" Maddie hadn't

seen her on-set for hours. She wondered if the guards at the gates had? Or had Evie DuLaps snuck onsite again?

"Yes, a gossip writer, so she should know."

"I know who she is. I'm just surprised she managed to get here so quickly after the—discovery."

Inspector Sadler gave a gruff cough. "She was found hiding under a pile of cushions in one of the dressing rooms in another bungalow. Says she saw nothing, of course, but no one saw her time of arrival. The guards say no one else arrived after you got here, at least by the main gates."

"So who *was* here this morning?" she said. But she knew the answer. Everyone.

Sadler glanced down at his notes. She tried to crane her neck to read them herself, but he turned the paper so she was blocked, the brute.

"Mrs. Bishop says she arrived with her husband shortly after dawn, but then when her last scene ended, she immediately left him to go study her scene in her dressing room," he said. Maddie nodded. "No one saw her there. But some people did hear her arguing with him last night at La Fonda. Not an unusual occurrence with those two, it seems."

"They weren't exactly the world's greatest lovebirds, I guess. Not that that's unusual with powerful couples like them."

"William Royle, working on revisions to the script.

Miss Lorelei Fontaine, er, keeping him company and working on costumes. Those two an item?"

Maddie was amazed Sadler was asking her opinion, and even being rather free with his own information. She wondered what was up. And she also didn't want to get Will into the soup. "I wouldn't know, Inspector, not being Evelyn DuLaps and thus up on my gossip."

He squinted at her across the table, and she gave him an innocent smile. "You were friends with Mr. Royle, I hear, back in New York."

"His family were neighbors."

"Cozy."

"I haven't seen him in years, so I don't know much about his love life."

"Think maybe Miss Fontaine was one of Mr. Bishop's squeezes? She sure wouldn't be the first. Mr. Royle might not have liked that."

Maddie doubted it. She remembered how Lorelei had expressed her dislike for Luther at the Hendersons' party. But she didn't want to get Lorelei in trouble, either, so she just watched Sadler coolly, trying to imitate her mother when she was freezing out some parvenu at the opera. "What does Lorelei say?"

"Says she was only the wardrobe designer, hardly worked with him at all."

A wardrobe designer who really wanted to be an actress—and was being thwarted by Luther Bishop. Just like Rex Neville with the movie in Germany he wanted to star in so very much. She shook her head. "Who else was here?"

"Hmm. Someone named Phil Ballard, second lead actor. The guards at the gate say he's a nice guy, a bit down on his luck until Bishop gave him a role. I can't see what he'd have against the man."

"Hmm," Maddie murmured. Phil *did* seem like a very nice guy. Also, a homosexual, and if Bishop knew that and was holding it over his head in some way—but she was getting carried away with suspicions, like she was in a detective novel or something.

"Rex Neville. The caterers who were setting up saw him go into his bungalow after his last scene. Though then he left for a while. Call of nature, I guess. Also, the head cameraman, a Bill Ackerman, working on a problem with some of the equipment in one of the workshops out past the orchard. Didn't even know anything was going on until we went out there and found him. Pretty cheesed to be interrupted. A few construction men, lads from Abiquiu, building that dumb fake homestead. None of them had ever met Bishop. And Miss DuLaps, whose only alibi is the dressing room cushions she was hiding under."

"Very interesting," Maddie murmured. And a puzzle with a lot of pieces. One totally unpleasant dead man who might or might now have killed himself, a big, spread-out set with lots of hiding places, and everyone around hating him. And most of them had been alone at the time of the murder, except Will and Lorelei.

Not to mention all the people who weren't on-set. Poor Maria Ortiz; Harry Kelly, the ousted actor. Maybe even gangsters wanting their loans called in, as Sadler said. There were valuable bootlegging pathways through this part of the desert; maybe someone didn't like the movie set getting in the way. And there were all those unfortunate girls Bishop chased, and their angry boyfriends and fathers.

Maddie sighed. The possibilities were large and baffling.

Sadler shuffled his papers. "Of course, we'll probably find he just offed himself. Drunk, maybe, or overdid it on the snow. These movie types are notorious for cocaine habits. Why can't they just stay in California and leave the rest of us alone?"

Maddie studied him carefully. He was being unusually communicative. She knew she should take advantage of it while she could. "Was contraband found on Mr. Bishop, then?"

Sadler scowled. "Not yet, but we haven't finished searching the place. There'll be an autopsy, of course, and an inquest."

Maddie wondered if David would be the doctor on duty for the autopsy, and could thus give her more information. "Am I free to go now, then? I can't think of anything else I can tell you at present."

"Sure." He waved her away, turning back to his papers. But as she gathered her handbag and gloves and rose to her feet, he suddenly looked back at her with his beady eyes narrowed.

"Don't go far, Mrs. Alwin," he said sternly. "And keep an eye on that flighty cousin of yours. If there's some sort of shenanigans going on around here, I'd wager she's right in the thick of it. Dames like that sort, you know . . ."

Maddie swallowed hard, suddenly half afraid he might be right. She gave him a short nod and hurried out of the stuffy little room. Gwen still sat with Will and Lorelei, the three of them playing a hand of cards. Bridget was sitting in a corner working, and Maddie could see Rex pacing and smoking past the window outside.

"Inspector Sadler says we can go now, Gwen," Maddie said, jerking on her gloves. "I say we should go to La Fonda. I'm aching to drown myself in a dulce de leche cake."

"Oh, yes," Gwen answered eagerly, jumping up from the table. She had powdered the traces of tears away and put on a coat of fresh lipstick, but her eyes still gleamed as if she was on the verge of tears. "But—Bridget told us we have to learn new scenes . . ."

She gestured weakly toward Bridget Bishop at her

table in the corner. Though she still wore her dressing gown, she was busily scribbling at a pile of papers, a fierce look of concentration on her fairy-face.

"The picture is already behind schedule, and someone has to manage things. Luther was hopeless, and now there will be a terrible scandal if we don't get ahead of things quickly," Bridget muttered. She glanced up at Gwen and frowned. "But you do look done in, Gwendolyn dear. Go eat something, get some rest. This will all look so much better in the morning. Will, do be a lamb and help me with this scene. It's an utter shambles!"

So much for the grieving widow, Maddie thought as she watched Bridget plow through the pile of scripts. But who could blame her, really? Luther Bishop had been no great spousal prize. Still, Maddie felt a sour pang of queasiness to think of what had happened so close by only hours before, and Bridget and the others seemed to have mostly forgotten a man had just been hanging there.

Will gave her a grimace and said, "Just take my car back to town, Maddie, and I'll fetch it later."

Maddie found Juanita outside, and they led Gwen to where the car waited under the trees. Gwen *did* look done in, much too pale under her powder and lipstick, and Maddie intended to call David as soon as they got home.

The sky soared overhead, a gorgeous, clear turquoise, not a cloud in sight, and the sound of hammering and shouts as the set went on being built made everything feel just that more unreal. Maddie glanced at the cliffs, all mother-of-pearl and coral in the sunlight, and remembered the ghostly looking figure she thought she had seen up there just before she went in search of Gwen—and found the body.

CHAPTER 9

"Are you sure you feel all right, Gwennie?" Maddie asked, putting a cup of tea down on her cousin's nightstand. It had been a long, sleepless night for all of them, and in the late morning Gwen was still bundled up in her bedspread. She had refused breakfast, and her elfin face was very pale except for the deep-purple shadows under her eyes.

Maddie could hardly blame her. Seeing an old flame, no matter how odious, pop up dead in such a gruesome way had to be a terrible shock, to say the least. She also worried about Inspector Sadler's words, warning her to keep an eye on her "flighty cousin" and to make sure neither of them went anywhere. It seemed he had found the death as suspicious as she herself did after a night of heavy thinking.

David had stopped to see Gwen on his way to the hospital, where in the absence of his friend Dr. McKee, the coroner, who was off on a case in Farmington, he had had to perform Bishop's autopsy before an inquest could be held. He'd said Gwen just desperately needed some rest, but Maddie wasn't sure that was all there was to it. Gwen seemed so agitated, her fingers with their chipped nail lacquer plucking at the covers, her gaze far away.

"I'm fine, Madkins, just a bit knackered," Gwen said. She smoothed down the crumpled blanket and reached for the tea, but her hand trembled. "Your yummy Dr. Cole said so himself. I'll be totally the elephant's elbow after a little nap. Hopefully the filming will be up and running again soon, and I can forget everything else by working."

Maddie wondered if filming would really be able to resume. Surely everything would in chaos! And there was something Bridget Bishop had hinted of, about getting ahead of "the scandal," that itched at her mind. She had read in the movie mags about the death of William Desmond Taylor, so sordid, so full of speculation. It had ended the career of several actresses. Maybe Bridget was worried about something similar.

"Oh, Gwennie, are you sure you should even go back there? It could be frightfully upsetting. And will they really resume shooting after—everything?"

Gwen took a long sip of the tea before answering, "Of course they will. Bridget won't give up the money *The Far Sunset* could bring, and she won't want to waste what it costs to keep us all idle, either. I'm sure she'll take it all over now. It's what she always wanted."

Maddie tidied up Gwen's dressing table as her thoughts raced. It was true Bridget seemed eager to take over the work, and she wasn't exactly the weeping widow. Could she plow through via sheer bloody-mindedness and pick up the reins? And what lengths would she have gone to in order to do that, really?

Gwen had left a messy jumble in front of the mirror, just like the makeup tables on set. The mirror itself was almost covered with a drape of scarves and a stray silk half slip. There was a tangle of jewelry, lengths of beads, a gold clip shaped like a leaf, emerald earrings. Half a bottle of her Jicky perfume was uncapped, sending a whiff of its distinctive spicy-woodsy lavender-vanilla scent into the air. A crystal pot of powder was spilled and a gilded tube of lipstick left open. Maddie wound it down, noticing the rosy-red color, the tip flattened from lots of use.

She thought of the glasses outside Luther's office, one lipstick stained with just such a rose. But it also looked like Bridget Bishop's shade, and Lorelei's too. Maddie turned it over and read the label. Elizabeth Arden, Ravishing Rose.

She recapped it, put the champagne cork–shaped top back on the Jicky, and set them on the mirrored dressing tray. "Maybe you're right. Maybe Bridget will want to work, too, to forget. Work can be a great comfort," she said. She had found it so herself. Painting had saved her, painting and the grand sweep of the New Mexican desert and the blinding sun, when nothing else could. But then she had loved Pete. She wondered about the Bishops.

Gwen seemed to agree with such nagging doubts, as she gave a disdainful little snort. "Well, as long as she doesn't fire me and recast my part, she can work for whatever reason she likes. We've all been such fools for too long, I say. Luther was absolutely rotten."

Maddie thought of Sadler's warnings. She hadn't seen Gwen in a long time, and so much seemed to have happened to her. She had been furious with Luther. "Gwen . . ." she said carefully. "You didn't—do something?"

Gwen gave her a wide-eyed stare. "Of course not! Too much trouble." She leaned back against the pillows and sighed. "Besides, I didn't have to, did I? Turns out he did it himself."

Gwen declared she would take a "wee sleepie" now, and as she pulled the covers over her head, Maddie closed the drapes over the window, shutting out the piercing Santa Fe sunlight. She gently shut Gwen's door and made her way to the kitchen, where Juanita was packing a picnic basket for David's lunch. She always worried he didn't eat properly, living in a rooming house on Alameda Street and working all the time. She was convinced he looked too thin when he stopped by to check on Gwen, but Juanita thought that about everyone.

"Is Señorita Gwen sleeping?" Juanita asked, pouring tea into a thermos.

"Yes. Hopefully she won't wake up until I'm back from the hospital."

"Don't worry, Señora Maddie. I'll keep an eye on her. To see such a death . . ." She shivered and touched the small silver cross she always wore around her neck.

"Yes," Maddie whispered, thinking of when Tomas Anaya died so horribly, and how the sight still haunted her nightmares. "How are *you* feeling after everything that's happened?"

"There's been too much death lately, too much evil. I will go talk to Father Malone this evening."

"Good idea." Maddie thought of the kind, twinkly-eyed Irish priest, and how helpful he had been when Tomas died. She had liked him very much, and he reminded her of Father Brown in the Chesterton novels she loved so much. "Do ask him to dinner here soon! I'd rather like to talk to him myself."

"I certainly will." Juanita put the last of the paper-wrapped sandwiches into the hamper. "Tell Dr. Cole to eat all of this. I put one of my plum tarts in here, and he loves them. He does look tired. Working so much lately . . ."

"I will watch him eat it myself," Maddie promised as she pinned on her straw cloche hat. She took the basket and impulsively kissed Juanita's cheek, causing her to give a startled laugh. Juanita was usually so reserved, so careful, but Maddie feared she was right—there had been too much evil lately. They all had to appreciate their friends even more. "I don't know what I would do without you, Juanita."

There was a knock at the door. Maddie glanced curiously back at Juanita. "Are we expecting anyone?"

"Not at this time of day," Juanita said. "The dairy has already made its delivery."

They hurried through the sitting room to the front door, and Maddie silently prayed it wasn't the police arriving with yet more bad news or anything like that.

But when she opened it, she saw not Inspector Sadler's portly self but Francisco Altumara, dressed in a very handsome gray suit and burgundy tie. His glossy dark, silver-touched hair was brushed back into a queue, and in his hands he held a black bowler hat and a bouquet of yellow flowers.

"Good afternoon, Mrs. Alwin," he said with a wide, gleaming white smile. Maddie could see why the man was in the movies; he was beyond handsome with that charmer's smile. "I've come to call on Juanita—Mrs. Anaya, that is. To see if she's recovered from what's happened. I haven't been able to stop worrying about her."

"How very kind of you, Mr. Altumara," Maddie answered. She glanced back at Juanita, who was trying to hide in the shadows. But she couldn't hide the flush of her cheeks. Maddie ignored the little shooing motion Juanita was trying to make with her dish towel and turned to smile back at Francisco. "As a matter of fact, Mr. Altumara, she *is* at home to visitors today . . ."

★ ★ ★

The day was a bright, beautiful, achingly clear one, such a contrast to the dark, disturbing events at the movie set. There wasn't a cloud in the blue sky, and the sun shimmered on the red and pink and white flowers that lined the stone walls.

Maddie made her way through the ornate iron gates of the park next to the cathedral and then hurried along the pathway that led to the hospital. She dodged around children playing with their hoops and mothers gossiping on the benches, their laughter like music on the breeze.

St. Vincent's was an old, white brick Victorian building, three stories of immaculately clean windows, smelling of soap and antiseptic and mashed potatoes, filled with the bustle of efficient nurses and doctors in a rush. Including, somewhere in its tiled halls, David. Maddie hurried up the stone steps and into the lobby.

"Oh, hello, Mrs. Alwin," the nursing Sister at the

front desk said. "Here to see Dr. Cole? Shall I have someone fetch him? He's downstairs."

"I'll just pop down, then," Maddie answered. "I
brought him lunch."

"That's wonderful! Someone has to remind him to
look after himself," she said with a *tsk* and a shake of her
white-capped head. She sounded so much like Juanita that
Maddie almost laughed—but then a flash of worry took
over. *Was* David making himself ill with working too
much? "We couldn't do without him here, being so short-
handed. And now he's filling in for Dr. McKee, too!"

"No," Maddie agreed. "We can't do without him."
And she feared that was becoming all too true. The
thought of David made her feel giggly as a schoolgirl,
giddy—and scared, too.

She went to press the button on the lift and had to
steady herself. It was a grim task ahead of her. She really,
really didn't like going to the basement.

When she stepped off the lift onto the concrete floor,
the cold, clammy air made her shiver, and there was no
light from the high, narrow windows that looked onto
the sidewalk above to warm things up. All the doors leading off the vestibule were closed, and she truly didn't want
to know what was behind them.

"David?' she called, her voice echoing in that terrible
quiet. "It's me, Maddie. The nurse said you were here."

"Back here," he answered, his voice sounding strained.

But maybe it was just the way the stone walls echoed and reverberated.

Maddie left the hamper on a table and hurried toward the back room, rushing so she wouldn't lose her courage. She never wanted David to think she was a piker!

He was washing his hands at a metal sink, his shirt-sleeves rolled up to reveal his strong forearms, sprinkled with sun-golden hair. His white coat was on a hook nearby. Maddie swallowed hard and glanced at the stone slab in the center of the sloped floor. She couldn't even start to face the racks of instruments that looked like something stolen from the Inquisition.

Not that the lumpy white sheet was any better.

"All done?" she said.

"Yes. Mostly healthy, as I thought, strong heart and lungs, though the liver was getting a bit fatty. We'll know more after toxicology is done." He frowned as he dried his hands. "But it was still very—odd."

Maddie didn't like the sound of that. Surely "odd" wasn't what one wanted in an autopsy. "Straightforward heart attack" seemed more like it. But the detective story reader in her was curious. "How so?"

"Well, it was a terrible hanging job, if you ask me. Very sloppy," he said.

"Is that so strange? He was no professional executioner. It must be a tricky thing."

"To be sure, and potentially a very painful thing. I

would think the man would be a little more careful. The knot wasn't even tied right; the neck wasn't broken. And the necktie that was used as a noose wouldn't have been efficient at all."

Maddie felt suddenly very queasy. "You mean he just—dangled there? Suffocating?"

"You would think so, but there aren't really signs of such a struggle." When David got deeply involved in his work, he seemed to forget everything else, and his enthusiasm took over. He always managed to carry Maddie along with him, even when that enthusiasm was for something like a gruesome hanging. He pointed out places on the sheet-draped figure. "There *are* bruises on the chest and upper shoulders, here and here, but nowhere else. I also found an excretion from the mouth that dripped down to the jaw, which sometimes happens at the moment of death when the jaw slackens." He gestured to the head area. "If a person is lying down."

"Could it be from when he hanged himself?" Maddie asked, half hoping that this was not what she feared. Not murder. But she remembered the stool, kicked away in the wrong direction, and feared her suspicions had been right. "Maybe he got good and drunk to steel himself up to it?" She thought of the glasses of whiskey, but there had been two of them.

David looked doubtful. "I don't think that was it. There was also this." He drew the purplish-white arm from under the sheet and showed her two tiny pinpricks on the inside of the elbow.

Maddie had a flash of the group she had seen that day at La Fonda. Elizabeth Grover and the movie people, and Elizabeth's forays into cocaine recently. "Film types do get into drugs quite a lot."

"Very true. But if he did, he's no habitual user. No track marks but these, no obvious signs on the internal organs. We'll have to wait for the blood test to see what's really in his system. I suspect, though, he was already dead when he was strung up."

★   ★   ★

Outside the cool, antiseptic-smelling hospital, Maddie was almost startled to see that the day was going on just as usual. People hurrying past on errands, children shrieking and laughing as their parents called to them to slow down, the sun shimmering on the pale-tan adobe walls, dogs barking, a car horn honking just beyond the park gates.

She slipped on her tinted glasses against the glare of the midday light and went down the stone steps into the park, hardly seeing the towering trees against the sky, the dappled shadows in golden sunlight on the path. Luther Bishop's ugly demise was like a bad dream that kept looping through her mind as if it was a reel of one of his own films. But it was all too real. The hanging body, the pinpricks on his arm, the unbroken neck . . .

She turned out of the park gates and went past the cathedral, a reassuring point of honey-colored stone beauty, serene and sure against the blue sky. Maddie could usually take comfort in the sight, her artist's eye reveling in the perfect harmony of the symmetrical, square towers, the juxtaposition of the subdued colors of the stones and the vivid stained glass, but today she barely saw it as she turned her back to its beauty and hurried toward the plaza.

So, someone really could have murdered Luther Bishop. She had hoped not, half hoped he *had* offed himself, even though he didn't strike her as the melancholic, self-defeating type. David's conclusions made too much sense, and he had seen too much death, both in the war where he'd been field medic and after, to make such mistakes. It seemed someone had drugged Bishop, killed him with either the overdose or strangulation, and found a way to string him up.

The idea of such a chaotic, dramatic ending made her shudder. What sort of person could bring themselves to plan and carry out a scenario like that? Someone in the theater, maybe, and there was no shortage of that around at the moment. No shortage of people who disliked Bishop, either. In fact, was there anyone who *didn't* hate the man?

Maddie paused at the corner and glanced back at the hospital. It, too, looked quiet and serene in the distance, its turmoil and emotion hidden behind pale Victorian walls. Yet she knew it was all there. David, too, had looked a bit disturbed as she left him, quiet and distracted as he kissed her cheek and promised to eat Juanita's lunch. Was it just the puzzle of the strange discoveries he had made, the gray shadow passing over their beautiful Santa Fe world? Or something more, maybe some bad memory? For she was sure he had them, secret memories of war and epidemics he didn't share. That sort of thing, hidden horrors, lives torn apart never to be the same again, was just a part of life now. Of everything around them since the war.

How well did she know him, really? How well could anyone know another person?

Maddie spun around and dashed down the block, past the balconies of La Fonda, where the carved doors opened and closed on guests going about their business. She made her way to the plaza, not sure where she was actually going, just needing light, air, and the distraction of other people.

"Madeline!" she heard someone call. She turned to see Alice Henderson hurrying toward her, her blue-and-green coat and matching feathered hat as bright as the day but her eyes full of worry. "My dear, it is true? Is Luther Bishop really dead?"

News did fly around their supposedly sleepy little town, Maddie thought. "Yes, I'm afraid so."

"And did he really kill himself?" Alice gasped. "It

seems so strange. He was just at our house, of course! I would never have thought him the sort to do such a thing. Much too full of himself."

"I would have said the same," Maddie said. She wasn't sure how much she should reveal, how much she should keep to herself for the moment. "But I guess we can't always know what's going on in someone's secret soul."

Alice sighed. "Much too true. That's what art is for, I suppose, to make such an attempt. But it will always be a feeble try." She paused with a frown, her gloved hands clutching at her beaded handbag. "I heard you were at the movie set when it—happened?"

"I took my cousin Gwen there, yes."

"What were your observations of it all? Not just poor Mr. Bishop, but how matters are progressing in general. I know little of that business."

"What do you mean, progressing?"

Alice leaned closer and said quietly, "I have been a bit concerned. William was so eager to invest in that project. He's so enthusiastic about art in all forms, you know, and the idea of a film made practically in our own back garden was too much to resist. But I was never sure. It's all so new, so uncertain. Then again, all art is a risk."

"That is true." Maddie thought of the set, all the constant movement and noise that seemed to move things forward only inches. But like Alice, she didn't know much about movies. "I'm afraid I wasn't there very long, and I have no idea how filming is meant to go. It seemed rather stop-and-go, not like a play, but surely it's always that way. It certainly looks like a high-quality project. I'm sure Mr. Henderson's investment is safe enough." Or had been, until the director died, of course.

Alice shook her head. "If only he hadn't put in quite so much. I'm afraid that enthusiasm got the better of him. I was worried about the schedule, and now of course there will be a scandal. I worry our investment will be quite swallowed up, and I'm sure there are plenty of others in the same position."

Maddie nodded, remembering stories of fired actors and replaced producers, of studios and investments. "I think Mrs. Bishop intends to take over the production. She doesn't seem like the sort to let a little scandal stop her."

Alice gave a little smile. "No, indeed. Well, I have to say that is an interesting development. A lady director! I'll have to call on her soon. How intriguing."

When they parted with promises to meet soon for lunch at La Fonda, Maddie still didn't feel like going home. She was afraid the gory thought of Luther Bishop's demise would be lurking in every quiet corner of her life, and being able to concentrate on painting seemed like a distant idea at the moment. She headed across the plaza to Mrs. Nussbaum's tearoom for a pot of Earl Grey and a plate of sugary cinnamon toast to build up her energy.

The shop was its usual cozy self, all white wicker furniture and potted palms, the windows draped in lace like a "ladies who lunch" spot in New York, and Maddie found a quiet table in the corner. But even there she couldn't escape the movie set. Evelyn DuLaps sat in the opposite corner, the droopy geraniums on her tall-crowned hat bobbing as she scribbled in a notebook. She glanced up and frowned as she saw Maddie watching her.

Maddie wondered what secrets were contained in that battered notebook. She gave the woman a bright smile and said, "Miss DuLaps, isn't it?"

"Who are you?" Evelyn replied, her frown deepening. "Haven't I seen you somewhere?"

"I'm Madeline Alwin. I believe we met on the film set." *Met*, of course, was a bit of an exaggeration, as Maddie had only seen Evelyn lurking about there, and then tossed out by Luther Bishop.

Evelyn tilted her head. "You're related to Gwendolyn Astor, aren't you?"

"She's my cousin."

"So, you're an Astor yourself! Imagine that. I hope you're not as scandalous as your cousin. She has so many romances, even I can't keep them straight." Evelyn gave a cackling laugh.

Maddie frowned. "I don't know about that."

"Is it true, then? That old Bishop is dead, like those cops said?"

"I'm afraid it is."

Evelyn scooted closer, her irritation seemingly forgotten. "Were you there, then, Miss Alwin? My readers would certainly love some firsthand information."

"It's Mrs. Alwin. And I doubt I know anything your readers would be interested in. I didn't see much." Maddie gestured to the notebook. "But I bet *you* have lots of juicy information right there. Information the police might like to know?"

Evelyn snapped the notebook closed and stuffed it in a battered old carpetbag. "It's just gossip. Nothing official for anyone like the police." She abruptly jumped up and dashed out of the tearoom, as if the word *police* was a curse. The doorbells jangled behind her.

Maddie sighed and slumped back in her wicker chair. It would be nice if she could get a bit more information from someone like Evelyn DuLaps, but then again, the woman was a pro who knew not to give anything away for free. Wouldn't hurt to try later, though.

Maddie suddenly felt so heavy, her mind foggy, as if the weight of everything that had happened had suddenly dropped down on her like a sandbag. She was sure she never wanted to hear the name Luther Bishop again.

And yet—she had to admit she was cat-killingly curious about what had happened. And what Evelyn DuLaps might be harboring in that notebook. It was probably terrifically juicy.

She had just tucked gratefully into her plate of cinna-mon toast when the doorbells rang again, and the last person she would have expected to see in a tearoom appeared. Inspector Sadler swept off his bowler hat and glanced around uncertainly.

To Maddie's surprise, he stopped right beside her table. "Mrs. Alwin," he said gruffly.

"Mr. Sadler," she answered uncertainly. "I—would you care to sit down and have some tea?"

"No, I only stopped in to get some cakes to take back to the station." Maddie had to admit she was a little sur-prised—he didn't seem the sort to be taking in treats to the office. "But I thought I'd have a quick word with you about the Bishop business."

"Really, Inspector? Me?" She'd thought he wanted her nose out of any police business. He'd made that clear.

He cleared his throat. "I know we didn't see eye to eye on the Anaya case, but you seem like—well, a nice lady. I just wanted to give you a little word of warning."

"Warn me?" Maddie whispered. The cinnamon toast she had eaten suddenly seemed to stick like sawdust in her throat.

"Yes. I know your cousin Miss Astor is staying with you. You might want to keep a close eye on her."

"And why is that?" Maddie asked, thinking of Gwen's erratic behavior lately, her tearful eyes, her wild smiles.

Things like that wouldn't go unnoticed in a small place like Santa Fe, especially not with a spicy murder on the go.

"Well, these movie actresses aren't always the most respectable, are they? It looks like she and Mr. Bishop weren't as professional together as they should have been. You're a widow, with your own home, your own work. Can't be too careful, can you?"

Before Maddie could answer, Mrs. Nussbaum came out with the delivery boxes for Inspector Sadler. He nodded to Maddie, put his dreadful hat back on, and left, the doorbells jangling behind him.

"Oh, Gwennie," Maddie murmured. "What have you done?"

CHAPTER 10

If Maddie had wondered if Luther Bishop's death would put a damper on filming, or even end up shutting it all down, she saw that was very wrong as they arrived on set the next day. In fact, she had never seen anything busier. It was almost like Grand Central Station at nine o'clock on a Monday morning.

Even more crew members swarmed around the wagon set, hammering, shouting, hauling away buckets and making mysterious piles of bricks and stones. Several girls in pink smocks rushed around, waving powder puffs and mirrors as they checked the effects of sunlight on cheekbones. Maddie glimpsed Francisco having his hair pomaded, and she waved at him.

"Look, Juanita, Francisco is here today," she said, pointing him out. He gave a beaming smile at the sight of Juanita. "He seems happy to see you again."

Juanita gave him the tiniest wave in return, blushing

a little as she turned to fiddle with the clasp on her hand-bag. "He's probably just happy to be working today. No time for mourning?"

"Oh, I told you Bridget wouldn't let any grass grow under her feet," Gwen said. She didn't look nearly as enthusiastic as Francisco. In fact, she was rather pale, her eyes shadowed as if she hadn't slept much the night before despite Juanita's plying her with warm milk. "I bet this flick will be in the can before you can say *cut*. We have to get paid before the studio honchos decide to pull the plug, you know."

"Oh, Gwen, there you are!" Bridget called, emerging from the throng of makeup girls with Will trailing behind her. He looked exhausted, but she looked like she was utterly bursting with her own source of sunlight. Her arms were full of typewritten pages, and she wore a smart dark-blue suit piped in white, a wide-brimmed hat on her bright hair. "I need you to look at these new scenes Will finished last night! You are in the first one up for today, and I think we are going to need to redo the ending of the arrival scene just a bit, too. Everyone needs to know the changes as soon as possible."

Gwen stared numbly down at the pages Bridget pushed at her. "Is my part going to be bigger, then?"

"Oh, yes. There's so much potential there, don't you think? You have a new little romance. Be sure and pay close attention to this scene here. I've just sent a telegram to Marcus Whiting, asking him to come out here and play your adoring swain. Wouldn't that be fabulous?"

"Marcus Whiting?" Gwen gasped. "But he's so—so . . ."

"Scrumptious looking? Yes, I know, and such an up-and-comer," Bridget said with a laugh. "Audiences do like a cute young couple to sigh over. I've also added a part for Lorelei as your sister; she's been wanting to give it a go for so long. Pictures need as many actresses as possible these days. No one wants to watch actors chest-thumping for twelve reels, do they?"

"Speak for yourself, darling," Phil Ballard called. He sat under the shade of a large umbrella, a stack of papers on his lap as two girls applied rouge and powder. It looked like Gwen wasn't the only one with new scenes to learn.

Bridget ignored him and spun Gwen around by the shoulders to give her a little push toward the bungalows. "Go on now, get to work! No time to lose. Will, do show her where to find Lorelei, and go over the scenes with them."

"Of course," Will said. "Hi, Maddie, good to see you! Don't stick around too long or Bridget will shove you onto the set, too," he called over his shoulders as he and Gwen hurried away. Gwen definitely looked a little perkier now.

"Oh, yes, indeed, very good to see you," Bridget said,

turning to Maddie and leveling her intense, bright-green gaze on her. It did feel a bit like being auditioned. Maddie could see how it would be hard to escape when caught in such energy and focus. What would Bridget Bishop do to get her own way? "We have enough actors, but have you thought more about art direction, Mrs. Alwin?"

"Art direction?" Maddie said. She had quite forgotten about that amid all the drama.

"You would be so perfect! You live here and know the landscape, *and* you're a real artist with a keen eye. I was watching the rushes, and I know we need to make things look a lot better in this picture. More authentically Western. Everything must be perfect! Dramatic and stormy, like it really is." She waved her arm at the sun-washed cliffs, the shimmering river, the dappled shadows of the trees. Her diamond bracelet, an elegant, distinctive pattern of fleurs-de-lis between oblong diamond baguettes, sparkled. "That's what would set us apart."

"But I have no idea what goes into making movie sets," Maddie said.

"Oh, easy-peasy. Here's the sketches we have so far for the scenes." Bridget took a few drawings from her stack of papers and pushed them at Maddie. "See what you think; look around the set. Think artistic! Big! Grand!" She whirled away and called, "Phil! No, don't run away now, I must talk to you . . ."

Maddie and Juanita stared after her in silence for a long moment. "Well. She is certainly—energetic," Juanita said.

"Yes," Maddie said with a sigh. "Wish I could bottle and sell it. Well, I guess I'll just have a look around the set, then. See if I can make things artistic."

"I'll go ask if the wardrobe girls need any help," Juanita said, and hurried off to the bungalows. Maddie wondered if she might just persuade Juanita to take Francisco a cup of coffee later, he was looking after her so wistfully.

She glanced down at the sketches of various set ideas and then over at the covered wagon and wall in the clearing by the river. She'd been given license by Bridget, seemingly the new director, to take a look around the set wherever she wanted. It seemed like too good a chance to give up to have a bit of a snoop around. She remembered what Sadler had said about Gwen, that the police had their eye on her cousin. If murder was indeed the verdict of the inquest, surely Gwen would be one of the first suspects, and Maddie had to help her.

She turned and started back toward the gate where Eddie's friend Harry was working again. When Tomas Anaya was killed, Harry had been one of the suspects, since he was always at the scene of the crime, and he was still always doing odd jobs, including bootlegging. But his sister June, who worked as a chambermaid at La Fonda, had told her Harry was on the straight and narrow now, working legit jobs and saving money. Maybe he had seen something interesting at his post.

He was leaning on the gate, talking to a girl in a brown smock from the tea tent.

"Oh, hi there, Mrs. Alwin," Harry said, standing up straighter when he saw her coming. He quickly smoothed down his rumpled hair. "Is there a problem on the set?"

"Not at all. You're obviously keeping the riffraff out quite handily," Maddie said as the girl hurried away. "I just wanted to see how you were doing after the terrible events. "

"Thanks, Mrs. Alwin," he said. "You're awfully nice to ask."

Maddie studied the road that snaked past the gate to the set, and she could see the tin roofs of the bungalows, the looming cliffs. "You have to clear everyone for entry here, don't you, Harry? This fence goes all the way around the set?"

"Oh, yeah," Harry said proudly. "We have to know everyone by sight, or they have to have a pass signed by Mr. B. Mrs. B now, I guess."

"Do you remember who all was here before Mr. Bishop died?"

Harry frowned in thought. "The Bishops, they were the first. Mr. Ballard, Mr. Royle, Lorelei and a couple of her wardrobe girls. I can check the log book to make sure."

"And were you at the gate the night before, too, when everyone left after filming?"

"Nah, I mostly work days. Ralph and his brother are on nights. Better them than me. Too spooky out here in the dark with just flashlights."

So there could have been people who stayed on set all night without being seen. "Who usually arrives here first?"

"Mr. Bishop used to, with his wife a little later. She usually drove in with Miss Fontaine, Mr. Neville, or sometimes Mr. Royle. The caterers are always early, with their vans; they come from La Fonda's kitchens. And then the extras in buses. And Mr. Ballard. He was usually the last of the principles to get here."

"The last, was he?"

"Bishop didn't like it, but Mr. Ballard didn't care two figs about it," Harry said with an admiring laugh.

"And that was usually it for the day?" Maddie asked.

"Till the mail truck gets here."

"Do they not get their mail at the hotel?" said Maddie.

Harry shrugged. "June, my sister, she still works at La Fonda, says only their personal stuff comes through the office. The mail room would get swamped with all the fan mail, and Mr. B likes his business stuff here where he can—could—get to it right away. The errand boys meet the mail truck and hand it all out."

Maddie remembered the young boy with the stacks of

letters and wondered if all the threatening notes had been hidden among them. "And that's all?"

"Sometimes the caterers bring in another van at noon, if there's a big scene with lots of extras," Harry said. "But not much else until the evening, once it's all set up and moving."

Maddie studied the road that looped away from the gates and down the hill. "Does anyone else ever try to get in? It seems so isolated."

Harry laughed. "Sure they do. Plenty of movie fans all around here, just like in any town. Lots of girls wanting to see Rex Neville. There were even a bunch of 'em in uniforms from the Loretto school. I bet the Sisters wouldn't like that."

Maddie hoped Ruby and Pearl weren't among them. They did seem young to have pashes, but one never knew. "Do you remember anyone else? Anyone suspicious at all?"

Harry frowned in thought. "There was one guy looking for his daughter. He was really angry we wouldn't let him in. He wouldn't leave. Luckily Mr. Ackerman, that big cameraman, was going past and helped us get rid of him," Harry said.

"Do you know who he was?" Maddie asked. "When he was here?"

"Two or three days ago? I think he's the fruit guy in town. La Fonda gets some of their produce from him."

Mr. Ortiz. "And was his daughter here?"

Harry shrugged. "If she was, she had a pass, or else she rode in on one of the cars. But I doubt it. I would have noticed a new, pretty girl."

So Mr. Ortiz had been there but had gone away again. Had he sneaked in again later? Or maybe someone else entirely?

"Is there another way onto the set?"

"I guess you could climb in over those cliffs, but that's miles away and a really steep path. And this fence goes all the way around the acreage rented to the movie company," Harry said. "Someone *could*, but it would take a while, I think."

Maddie nodded. The mail truck soon arrived, appearing from around the bend to the gates, and she followed it back to the main set. She watched as the errand boy who always ran around calling "Places!" came dashing by to help unload the burlap mail sacks. There were several, stuffed full, and she could see why La Fonda didn't want to get flooded with so many letters.

"Need a bit of help?" she asked, and the kid grinned at her.

"Sure! We just take 'em over there and sort them out by name. Mrs. B's secretary picks hers up at lunchtime."

"What happens to the others?" Maddie asked. She heaved up one of the bags and followed him into one of the smaller bungalows. Somehow, he managed to carry two, despite his diminutive size.

"I take 'em around and leave them on the desks and dressing tables, if they're filming." He dumped the bags out onto a long table and started sorting them into boxes labeled with names. Rex Neville definitely *did* have the most.

Maddie didn't remember seeing much discarded mail in Luther's office, except for the threat note. Yet there were several letters for him now, most with the studio's logo on the return address. "What did Mr. Bishop do with all this? His office seemed too tidy to hold so many envelopes."

The boy glanced around, his eyes wide. "He had me take it to his secret office, miss. He only trusted me, you see."

"Secret?" Maddie whispered back, intrigued.

"Well, I mean, not *hidden* or anything. Folks knew about it. He went to watch the rushes there. But he kept it locked. I just had to leave the mail outside the door." He held up a letter with a scowl. "I guess we should just give 'em to Mrs. B now."

"He must have trusted you a lot to have you deliver to a secret office," Maddie said carefully. "Was it hidden in his real office, behind a wall or something?"

He laughed. "That sounds like a movie. Some haunted-house flick or something. No, it was just a little room, kinda like a closet, in the bungalow behind the makeup room."

"I see. How clever." Maddie put a few more letters into Luther Bishop's box, but she saw nothing that looked like the short, rough threat note. Why would anyone send them through the post, though, if they knew Luther was already dead? And what if they hadn't gone through the post at all but had been hand delivered?

They soon had the bags sorted, and the boy gathered all the boxes except the Bishops'. Maddie saw there were a few letters for Gwen, and she tucked them into her jacket pocket. "I'll drop these by for Miss Astor. She's my cousin."

"Jeepers!" the kid exclaimed. "Are you an actress, too? Have I met you here on set, miss, or seen you in a flick? You all look so different without your makeup."

Maddie laughed. "No, I'm not an actress. Just an artist. A painter." Speaking of which, she had an actual artistic job to get on with now. But surely it wouldn't hurt to take one peek at this intriguing "secret" office?

It didn't take her long to find the doorway. It was where the kid had said—behind the makeup room, down a short, quiet hallway. Unlike the constant noisy bustle closer to the set, the narrow corridor was silent, almost spooky. The door was closed, half hidden in the gloomy light, but not locked. Maddie slipped inside and found a small, windowless room that already smelled musty with disuse. She flipped on a small table lamp and took a look around.

It appeared as if the police hadn't been there yet. Maybe Sadler didn't know about it yet, or maybe it hadn't seemed important if they were still officially treating the death as a suicide. The desk drawers were all neatly closed, nothing out of place.

Unlike Luther's more public office, where there were piles of scripts everywhere, this room was almost spartan. Except for the mailbox, the desktop was bare, the rolling chair pushed in neatly. A small table by the door held a lockbox. But there was a screen on one wall, with a projector and sofa set up facing it, like a tiny screening room. A few canisters of film were stacked beside the sofa.

Maddie took a quick glance at the projector and couldn't figure out how it worked at all. If she wanted to actually watch the film, she knew she would have to recruit someone to help, and she wasn't sure who to trust. Just about everyone had had good reason to hate Luther Bishop. The labels on the canisters said just "TDD #1" or "#2," and there were only initials on the reels at the bottom of the stack.

She moved on to what she knew she *could* do on her own—snoop through desk drawers. Two of them were unlocked but yielded only packages of blank stationery and boxes of stuff like paper clips. The paper was thick and pure white, like the poison-pen notes, but also like almost all the other letters and bills. Not cheap, but common to every stationery shop.

The top and bottom drawers were locked. Maddie decided to try something she had read in a book and jimmied the top drawer open with one of the paper clips bent into a hook. It was shallow but wide, filled with letters. She sifted through them and saw that they were mostly love notes, signed with a myriad of names—Sylvia, Liz, Clara, et cetera. A few had lipstick kisses, more than one in Ravishing Rose. One was ripped in half, the signature gone. The handwriting was crooked and erratic, and Maddie could read a few words—*keep your promise; I know they're wrong.*

Feeling slightly queasy at the man's tomcat tendencies, she pushed the letters back into place. Shoved at the back of the drawer were a few more notes, and they were rather different. They were more threats, written in the same blocky, black handwriting.

There was a sudden burst of noise in the corridor outside. "Places on set!" someone shouted. "Hurry up, everyone!"

Maddie hastily stuffed the notes into her handbag, shoved the drawer closed, and turned out the lamp. There was no time to pick the lock on the bottom drawer; she could only pray there were no more notes there. If the police came back, she didn't want to face Sadler and tell him why she was snooping. He wouldn't listen to her, anyway.

But before she could slip out, she heard a rattle at the

door, and her breath caught in her throat. What if the killer had come back? And she was there, alone! There was no time to hide. The door opened, and Phil Ballard slipped inside. He scooped up the lockbox from a small table.

"Whatever are you doing?" she demanded, making herself stay firm, and braver than she felt.

Phil stumbled back a step, as if startled. He looked up, his eyes wide, and held out his empty hand, as if caught in a stickup in a mobster flick. A wire glinted between his gloved fingers, and she tried to hide her fear.

"Madeline! You scared the spit out of me," he gasped. "What are you doing here?"

"Snooping, of course. Gwen says you actors are very superstitious. Aren't you afraid of a—a death curse or something in here?"

Phil glanced around. "I don't *like* it in here, true. Gives me the heebie-jeebies. But I needed to find something before they closed up this room." He looked down at the box. "I heard the police might pack up everything and haul it away, and I was afraid they might open this up at the station. They seem to have forgotten it so far."

Maddie tiptoed closer to the table, keeping her eye close on him. "What's in it? Are you trying to rob the Bishops?"

"I'm not really sure what's in it. But there's something I need, and this seems like the most likely place for it—I hope."

Maddie studied the box, a plain, gray steel affair like something one could buy in any hardware store. "Here, let me see that," she said, holding out her hand for the wire. She slid it into the lock and carefully wiggled the end up under the mechanism. "You have to slip it under the catch and then pull up—like this."

The lock clicked open, and Phil's eyes widened in admiration. "How did you know that?"

"A book I found once in my brother's room when we were kids. He always did have a secret liking for detective novels and things like that. It seemed like fun to give it a try." She opened the lid and stared down at a jumble of papers. More threat notes, like in the drawer, or love letters? "What exactly are you looking for?"

Phil was quiet for a long moment. "You seem like a sophisticated sort of lady."

"Well—thank you," Maddie answered, a bit confused.

"So I hope you'll understand." He took in a deep breath. "I didn't really want to do this movie, at least not this part. Like the lovely Rex, I'm tired of being typecast, tired of doing the same sort of thing over and over. But while he is the matinee idol, I always seem to be the villain. I was done with that. But Luther had some—well, some photographs. I'm not proud of them. He used them to get me to take this part."

"Romantic photos?" she guessed.

Phil nodded grimly. "He said he would hand them

over when the picture wrapped and would say no more about them."

"You believed him?"

"I didn't have much choice, did I? Now I have to make sure no one else sees them. Especially not the police."

"I see." Maddie dumped out the papers in the box and they sorted through them. There were the usual things found in lockboxes—stock certificates, insurance policies, stuff she was sure Bridget would need. She glanced over one and saw it was a policy on the film itself, indemnifying against "acts of God," but the amount wasn't nearly enough to cover what Luther seemed to be losing. There were receipts for jewelry. Maddie saw one for three gold clips, and the diamond bracelet Bridget had worn at the Hendersons' party. Apology gifts?

At the bottom were a few envelopes filled with photos. Two of them had images of people she didn't know, but the next was what Phil was looking for. She glimpsed one of Phil wrapped in a blurry, blond man's arms before he gave a happy little cry and stuffed the envelope in his pocket. Together they sorted through the rest of them to be sure there were no more. There were none of Phil but a few of Rex, seemingly at a party, cocaine lined up on the table in front of him. Maybe the contract hadn't been entirely due to his agent's incompetence after all.

"It looks like Luther Bishop had a very lucrative second career as blackmailer," she said.

Phil chortled. "You could say that. He was very adept at digging up the dirt on everyone. Why do you think we all put up with him?"

Maddie frowned as she thought of all the various bits of scandalous information she had heard lately. It would take a lot of time and effort to organize such a flood of gossip and put it to good use. "That gossip writer, Evelyn DuLaps. Could she have helped him out?"

"I wouldn't be surprised. She was always hanging around the studio."

Maddie nodded, and scooped up the papers to put them back in the box.

"Do you think—think I might have killed him, then?" Phil asked, surprisingly timid for a tough-guy actor who always had to play the villain.

Maddie glanced up at him and saw the pain in his eyes. "I don't think I would blame you. Taking advantage of someone's most tender feelings is certainly despicable. And not the *only* despicable thing Luther Bishop did, to be sure."

"No." Phil sighed. "It's true I thought about how much easier my life would be if Luther just disappeared. But I'm afraid that despite my wicked screen persona, throwing impoverished widows off their land and such, I'm the most squeamish person you would ever meet. Couldn't even kill a mouse. I can't pretend I'm really sorry he's gone, but I couldn't have done it myself."

"I don't think you could, either," Maddie admitted. She had liked Phil from the start. He seemed so nice and easygoing, funny. She wouldn't have thought to introduce him to Gunther, her best friend, if she hadn't thought so. But people could be endlessly complex, and who knew what they could really do when under such terrible pressure?

She sorted through the rest of the papers. She caught a quick whiff of some faint scent from the folds of one of the notes. She didn't remember any smell from the other notes in the trash cans. Puzzled, she lifted it for a sniff—and froze in horror. It was the distinctly woody, sharp scent of Jicky.

Gwen wore the same lipstick as Bridget and several other ladies, the same lipstick found on the glass outside the office, but Bridget and Lorelei, wore Shalimar. Only Gwen wore Jicky. And surely Luther had known that, too. Was that why he kept the notes?

"What's that?" Phil asked.

Impulsively, Maddie stuffed the notes into her handbag. "I'm not really sure."

Phil scowled. "Oh, don't tell me he had something on *you*, too! The vile cad."

"No, not me. I just—I hate bullies."

"Don't we all?"

Maddie glanced around the room, so empty now, already musty with that disused, damp feeling. But it still seemed to echo with old horrors. She remembered what David had told her about how he died, what she had seen herself, and she studied the ceiling beam like the one where he had been strung up. They looked too flimsy to hold such weight, made to be temporary as they were.

She shivered and turned away. "Did you get everything, Phil?"

"I think so. Shall we get out of here? I feel quite oofy."

"You and me both."

They put the lockbox the way they found it and hurried out of the office, closing the door behind them.

"Will you stay with the movie now?" Maddie asked him as they hurried back to the very welcome light and noise of the makeup room. It felt like two different worlds, like Persephone hurrying out of the underworld into her mother's light-filled realm again, and it made Maddie's head swim.

Phil seemed to feel it, too. He sucked in a deep breath. "Oh, sure. I like Bridget, and I don't want to leave her stranded. But after this, I'm looking for different sorts of roles. Thanks for your help, Madeline. I guess you really are a sophisticated sort of young lady."

They stepped out of the building into the sunny day, the warm dry breeze. Phil was called away for a camera test, and Maddie took her tinted glasses out of her bag and slid them on as she studied the scene. Bridget was examining the lights again, and Bill Ackerman was walking toward his cameras. Juanita sat under the shade of the trees working on a blue costume coat for Rex, who was still reading his Goethe. She didn't see Gwen anywhere, but her bag with the notes felt like it weighed a hundred pounds.

Could Gwen have done it? Surely she was angry enough, hurt enough, by Luther's caddish behavior, and Maddie remembered how Gwen had always had a quick temper. Even when they were kids, Gwen had been swift to screaming anger, and just as swift to be sorry. But could she really, physically have done such a thing?

No one seemed to actually like Luther at all.

But that meant everyone else had just such grudges. Phil Ballard. Maddie did have the sense he hadn't done it, that he was telling the truth when he said he couldn't even hurt a mouse, yet he was an actor. An actor who was quite good at playing villains in his films. She could very easily be wrong about him. And there had been that photo of Rex and the drugs, too. Had Luther gotten him to back out of the German film he wanted to do so much by blackmail? And what about Evie DuLaps? Had she been feeding Luther gossip, the two of them pretending to hate each other when she snuck onto the set?

"Maddie, there you are!" she heard Bridget call. She turned to see the actress-director hurrying toward her.

She wore her white flannel dressing gown over her costume, but the diamond bracelet still flashed on her wrist, not at all the sort of thing a poor homesteading woman would wear. "What do you think of the setup for this scene? I want it to convey the vast sweep of the land, the dangerous impersonality of its beauty. Show what this family is really up against. It all feels sort of, I don't know, claustrophobic right now."

Maddie pushed away the thoughts of murder and blackmail swirling back and forth in her mind and made herself study the scene before her. It was true, work was always its own balm.

"Let's take a look from up there," she said, and she and Bridget headed up the rocky path to the top of the cliffs past the river. From up there, she could see the setup of the wagon, the walls, clearly. She remembered the figure she had glimpsed up there.

From up there, it all looked small, like a toy scattered with cameras, props, and people scurrying around in pale blurs.

"You could move the wagon over there closer to the water, with those hills in the distance. I don't know if your cameras could pick it up clearly, though," she said, pointing out a spot where the mountains made a purplish, dramatic backdrop. "Or there, close to the trees."

Bridget nodded and scribbled something down in a little, leather-covered notebook. It looked a bit like the ones Evie DuLaps carried around. In the unfiltered light of the mesa, Bridget was still beautiful but also pale, her eyes glittering.

"Are you feeling all right?" Maddie asked, wondering if she had been eating and sleeping enough.

Bridget laughed. "Just peachy. I just haven't been able to sleep very well. There's so much to catch up on, you know, and the hotel is so old and creaky."

"Oh, yes, I can see it's very busy."

"I want to get this film done soon, but as well as possible to show the studio I can do this as well as Luther. Much better, in fact." She tilted her head, frowning down at the busy set. "And if we can wrap before they hear too much . . ."

Maddie remembered the threat of scandal always hanging over everything. Scandal that seemed all too real. "You're worried about the gossip?"

Bridget sighed. "Of course. California is a long way away. I think we can hold off on telling all the details for a little longer. If the gossips are already here, though, we might not have much choice. We just have to work fast. I know I can do it."

"Have you always wanted to be a director, then?"

"Oh, no. Just an actress, from the time I was a kid at my grandparents' mortuary. I got my first part when I was just sixteen, a chorus girl in the Follies, even though I really wanted to do Shakespeare. Ran away from the convent to audition. That's how I met my husband, you see. He liked to lurk around the theaters, looking for girls who might look decorative on film."

"Wasn't he rather older than you?"

"Of course. That's how he liked them. Look at poor little Miss Ortiz. I hope her father is keeping her locked up tight. Even when I first met Luther, everyone said he was a creeper."

"And you—he . . ."

Bridget gave a bitter little laugh. She pulled her ivory holder and a pack of Chesterfields from the pocket of her dressing gown. "No, I thought I was better than all that. I held him off for quite a while, moved on from the Follies to do some serious theater. But I wanted to be in films so much I could taste it. And those convent lessons wouldn't quite leave me. So he married me. He'd never really been turned down, and it made him more determined." She lit up and took a deep drag, the smoke silvery around her beautiful head. "What a little fool I was. Trapped with him all these years."

"It sounds terrible," Maddie agreed. She wondered if Bridget knew about Gwen and the others, and was sure she did. How had she really felt about it all? How angry was she about her wasted years?

"I know," Bridget said with sudden brightness. "Let's have a picnic! It really is gorgeous out here, and we haven't had a chance to see it all yet. I think we could all use a treat after these horrors. And maybe we could get some inspirations for the set. You could tell us a good spot, couldn't you, Maddie?"

"Of course," Maddie answered. "A picnic is a great idea. There are lots of pretty spots in the mountains. Maybe . . ."

A sudden loud curse burst out below them, words so vile Maddie had sudden terrible memories of Nanny and washings-out of mouths with soap. Bridget frowned, and held her cigarette up to peer past the smoke to the set.

Bill Ackerman stood by his camera, his face red with fury. He threw his hat on the dusty ground, and everyone gathered around in fearful curiosity. Bridget ground out her cigarette and hurried down the path toward him, and Maddie scrambled to follow.

"What's wrong, then?" Bridget asked.

"That damned . . ." Bill growled. "Someone's been tampering with my camera! Look, the sprocket has been cut through and the film ruined."

"What!" Bridget cried. "How could that happen?"

"It could happen because your blasted husband put guards at the gate but not on valuable equipment, and this place is crawling with useless people," Bill said.

Bridget looked appalled. "How soon can it be fixed?"

"Not for a few days. I need to get the part, and I'm

sure no one around here has one." He glared around at the onlookers. "Did anyone see anything, then?" But everyone denied it.

"Is this going to cost us even more money?" Bridget demanded furiously. She threw her cigarette holder as hard as she could, a hail of curse words raining down. Bill ducked away. "I will find whoever is doing this, and they will be very sorry! Those pieces of shit."

"Is that how convent girls talk now?" Bill asked.

"It is now!" Bridget shouted. "Fix it! Immediately!"

CHAPTER 11

Maddie waited until they got home to confront Gwen about the notes. Juanita had gone to fetch the twins from school and run some errands, and Eddie was working at La Fonda, so the house was quiet.

Gwen flopped down as soon as they went inside, kicking off her shoes onto the sitting room rug. "Wow, what a day! You don't happen to have a teeny spot of gin tucked away somewhere, do you, Maddie?"

"No, I don't. But I do need to talk to you about something." Maddie pulled the notes out of her bag. "Did you write these, Gwen? Tell me the truth."

Gwen sat straight up and stared at the papers, open-mouthed. At first, her eyes widened innocently and she shook her head, making her silvery hair tremble as if she was in a movie scene of injured femininity. But Maddie just kept watching her, holding up the letters, and Gwen slumped back again.

"They smell like your perfume," Maddie said. "Surely you knew he would recognize it? Or maybe that's what you wanted."

"It wasn't my idea, not at first," Gwen said sullenly. "Luther got threats even before we left California. He was really angry about it, and I could tell he was scared, too, even though he tried not to show it. He was furious that he couldn't figure out who it was, and I thought I could just—add to it a bit. I was so angry with him. I just sort of slipped them in with the others. So many people hated him, what was one more?"

"But what if the police found these and traced them to you?" Maddie sat down beside Gwen, suddenly so weary. "Luther had them in his lockbox. Why would he keep them? The others were in the trash or stuffed in a drawer. Did he know it was you?"

Gwen shrugged. "He never said anything to me. Like I said, I just wanted to scare him a bit. I didn't realize I left some perfume behind, really, Mads. I'm not a professional threatener, after all."

"No, but it seems Luther was something of a professional blackmailer! Anyone threatening him is suspect now. Inspector Sadler is watching you, Gwennie. I'm very worried."

Gwen sniffled, her eyes glistening with tears. "How was I supposed to know Luther would end up dead? I didn't have anything to do with it! You believe me, don't you, Maddie?"

Maddie gave in and took Gwen into her arms for a hug. She *did* believe her. Like Phil Ballard, Gwen wasn't the killing sort. The angry sort, sure, but she couldn't keep a cool head long enough to plan a murder. "I do, but Sadler may not. It doesn't look good for him to have a Hollywood director dead on his doorstep. He'll be looking for any excuse to make an arrest."

"Surely I can't be the only suspect! Or even the main suspect. Besides, you have the letters now, not Sadler."

"Are these the only ones you sent, Gwen?"

"Yes."

"Are you sure?"

"Yes! I told you, Mads—I was hurt. Maybe I *felt* like killing him, but I could never have done it. You do believe me, don't you?"

Maddie rubbed at her temples, where a thumping headache was forming. She didn't really know what she thought anymore. The whole Bishop movie business was like a Chinese puzzle box, made of blackmail and hate and anger and greed and ambition she couldn't even unpack now. She certainly did want to believe it wasn't Gwen. They were cousins, closer than sisters once, and Gwen had always had such a sweet impulsiveness about her. It was hard to imagine her killing and stringing up a man. But anger and betrayal were such powerful things.

She looked at her cousin, and Gwen buried her hands in her face, sobbing. "Oh, Maddie. What if the inspector does think I did it? How did I get into this mess?"

Maddie's heart melted. She hugged Gwen again, feeling her cousin's whole, slight body shake with tears. "Shh, now, I'm sure everything will be okay. Like you said, lots of people hated Luther. Anyone could have done this. I know it wasn't you."

"Then we just have to—to find who it really was," Gwen gasped. "Like a detective novel!"

"Yes." If only it were that easy. Maddie studied a row of battered novels on her shelf, between the art books and Shakespeare. Mostly Chesterton and his detecting priest, but also several others—English spinsters, clever aristocrats, French gendarmes. Surely none of them had ever dealt with such a loathsome victim, or so many justified suspects? She sighed, and patted Gwen's shaking shoulder.

Maddie reached for her sketchbook. "Maybe you'd let me draw you, then? I'd love to do a portrait of you, Gwennie, and then you will be forced to sit still for a while!"

Gwen smiled. "Like when we were children?"

"Exactly."

Gwen settled herself on a chair near the sunlight streaming from the window. The glow turned her bright hair into a halo, and she did seem to settle as Maddie went about sketching out the first lines of a portrait. They chatted a bit about things that had nothing to do with the murders: fashion, cocktails, the newest plays in New York. It *was* almost like when they were children and wrapped up in their own world together, away from all that might harm them. They were only disturbed when Juanita and the girls got home, and Juanita went into the kitchen to check on her bread dough.

The peace did not last long.

Maddie heard a knock at the front door, but she went on sketching, sure it was a delivery from the dairy or something like that, as it was a strange time of day for visitors. David was usually busy with patients during the day, and the possibility of sending a book to the movies seemed to have jumpstarted Gunther's creativity. She went on sketching, absorbed in the lines and shadows of capturing an image, and was startled when Juanita appeared in the doorway.

Juanita twisted her hands in her apron, her expression full of worry. "Señora Maddie, Inspector Sadler is here," she whispered. "He says he must see Señorita Gwen at once!"

Gwen sat straight up, her eyes wide. "What . . ."

Inspector Sadler appeared behind Juanita, his bowler hat in hand, a scowl on his red face. "I'm sorry to intrude, Mrs. Alwin. But I'm afraid I'm here to place Miss Astor under arrest . . ."

CHAPTER 12

Maddie stared up at the plain stucco and brick-fronted building. It looked harmless, quiet, non-descript. Only the small, high, iron-barred windows revealed it to be the jail.

She took a deep breath and tugged at her kid gloves, straightened her hat. She had worn her most matronly outfit, a gray-and-white suit with matching felt hat, and her grandmother's double-strand pearl necklace. She had learned after dealing with the local law after the Anaya murder that a girl always needed to look respectable when visiting the jail.

Oh, Gwen, she thought sadly as she stared up at those barred windows. Gwen Astor wasn't used to such conditions; she was surely scared to death in there. Afraid she would be thought guilty—or maybe scared they would find out all about her and Luther Bishop. Maddie was determined to get her out of there as soon as possible.

She stiffened her shoulders and marched through the door. After the sunshiny day, the dimness seemed to wrap her up in inescapable stickiness, like a spider's web. The thick, stuffy air smelled of stale, fried food and wool uniforms that could use a washing. Maddie tried not to breathe too deeply and made her way to the counter, which was piled up haphazardly with papers. No doubt each one was a case just waiting to be solved.

The policeman who stood behind the counter, shuffling those papers around, looked familiar. Tall, skinny, his dark hair brilliantined to a patent shine, youthful acne still spotting his cheeks. Was he the same young man who had manned the station when Eddie was arrested? Maddie wondered why he hadn't been promoted by Sadler.

"Tony, isn't it?" she said, pulling off her gloves. "You're Harry's cousin, right?"

He straightened up and tried to look very official. It didn't quite work. "I—I am. Mrs. Alwin."

She gave him a sweet smile. "You remember me! Then I'm sure you know I'm here to see Miss Gwen Astor. My cousin."

Tony shifted on his feet, his face turning red. "Inspector Sadler said she's to be kept quiet. She's been—well, kinda hysterical."

"She *is* an actress, after all. Of course she would react that way to being falsely accused of such a terrible thing.

Mr. Springer, her attorney, is on his way, and would be most unhappy to hear she is being held in such isolation."

Tony swallowed hard. "You hired Frank Springer?"

"Of course. He is an old friend." That was a bit of an exaggeration. She had only met Mr. Springer, a legendary rancher, attorney, and politician in New Mexico, when he'd helped Eddie. But they *had* conducted a very interesting telephone conversation when she had asked him about Gwen. He seemed very keen to help a pretty young movie star. Maddie tapped her fingertips on the counter. "Now, Tony, may I see my cousin? I know you will help me; you are such a smart young man."

"Okay," he said reluctantly, reaching for a ring of keys. "But only for ten minutes. And don't tell the inspector. I'm sure tired of working this counter."

Maddie mimed zipping her lips and followed him past the counter and down a dark, narrow hallway past a series of heavy, locked doors with tiny, grilled windows. She held her breath against the smell of urine and bleach. She could hear the sound of retching from last night's drunks.

"My cousin is a *lady*," she hissed. "She should not be in here!"

Tony's face turned even more red, and if Maddie had been in a softer mood, she might have recommended some of Juanita's lavender salve. But she was in no mood to be helpful.

"There isn't anywhere else, Mrs. Alwin," Tony said sheepishly. "Inspector Sadler said . . ."

"There's house arrest," Maddie answered. "Where is she going to go? Flee into the mountains to live in a cave or something?"

"I don't know, Mrs. Alwin, really." Tony unlocked the last door in the row. "Ten minutes, remember?"

Maddie rushed through the door. It closed behind her with a clang, but didn't lock. At least Tony was *trying* to be nice.

The tiny, screened window near the low ceiling gave enough dusty light for her to see the stained concrete floor, the narrow bed with its rough gray blanket, a chair, a covered bucket in the corner for a toilet. Very far away from Fifth Avenue. And there was Gwen, huddled on the bed, the blue dress and coat she had left the house in rumpled, her short hair tousled, her cheeks streaked with tears.

"Maddie!" she sobbed. "I'm so glad you're here. Can I leave now?"

"Very soon, I'm sure. I've hired you the best attorney in the state, and he is on his way," Maddie answered, her heart aching to see her bright, vivacious cousin like that. If Luther Bishop wasn't already dead, she'd have been tempted to do it herself.

She put down the small suitcase she had brought,

filled with clean clothes, a hairbrush and tooth powder, a bottle of Jicky, and some of Juanita's pecan brittle candy, and sat down next to Gwen on the hard mattress. Gwen collapsed against her shoulder, and Maddie hugged her close.

She remembered when they were girls, how they would sit on Gwen's canopied bed and brush each other's hair, whispering hopes for the future. They had never included a jail cell.

Maddie handed Gwen a linen handkerchief. "It will be fine."

"Oh, Mads, I didn't do it," Gwen gasped. "You have to believe me."

"It would be understandable if you did."

Gwen looked up, her eyes wide with horror. "You can't think that, Maddie, please! I couldn't stand it if you, of all people, thought I could kill someone. It's true I hated him. If I'd known where to get a voodoo doll to stick pins in, I would have. But to string him up . . ."

"No, dearest. Of course not." Maddie looked down at Gwen's small hands, the chipped scarlet polish on her long nails. She really couldn't have. "But someone did it. Do you have any idea who? Did you hear anything onset, see anything suspicious?"

Gwen wiped her eyes and thought in silence for a long moment. "Not really. Anyone could have done it, really. No one liked him at all."

Maddie sighed. "So it seems."

"But if the police think *I* did it, they won't look any further!"

"Gwennie, listen to me, we don't have much time." Maddie held her cousin's shaking hands tightly. "Mr. Springer will be here soon to bail you out. Just read the movie mags I brought in your suitcase, sit tight, and don't worry. I am looking into matters."

"Mads, no." Gwen's nails dug into Maddie's hands. "It's so dangerous. If you're hurt because of this, because of *me* . . ."

"I won't be. Oh, Gwennie, I won't let an old heel like Luther Bishop ruin your whole life." She wouldn't let Gwen be another murder victim, either. Maybe jail actually was the safest place for her at the moment. "It will all be fine. Just stay calm, and for heaven's sake, spray some of your Jicky on these pillows. It will smell much better in here."

They had time for only one more hug before Tony came to kick Maddie out. She glanced back one more time at Gwen from the doorway and saw her cousin taking the bottle of perfume and the bag of Juanita's candy from the suitcase. She already looked calmer. Maddie just wished she could stay that way herself.

The bright day outside, brimming with the smell of fresh, green late-summer air, the noise of regular life, was sort of a shock after the dank dimness of the jail.

Maddie tilted the brim of her hat against the light and strode off down the street, more determined than ever to make sure Gwen was out of that place soon. That her life and career would not be ruined by one mistake with the likes of Luther Bishop. An ill-thought affair did not make a murderer.

She crossed the plaza toward Kaune's grocery store, deciding that maybe baking her one recipe, currant scones (though she could also do scrambled eggs in a pinch), would help her think a bit more clearly. Juanita usually didn't like anyone else using her kitchen—she was so sure people always misplaced things—but Maddie knew she wouldn't mind this once.

"Mrs. Alwin!" she heard someone call out. "How are you today?"

Maddie turned to see Father Malone hurrying toward her down the sidewalk. In his black cassock and wide-brimmed black hat, his height and girth, he should have been an intimidating character. But he couldn't be even if he tried, not with his rosy, plump cheeks and eyes shining with Irish humor and curiosity behind his spectacles. He had been a good friend and counselor to Juanita, and a great help in finding Tomas Anaya's killer. Plus, he also enjoyed a good detective novel.

"Oh, Father Malone, how glad I am to see you!" she answered. "I'm in such a pickle."

His merry smile turned serious, and he gave her a

solemn nod. "Yes, I had heard there was a terrible event at the movie set. I do hope you and Mrs. Anaya are recovering? Such a dreadful thing to see, and so soon after Mr. Anaya."

"And I'm afraid that's not all," Maddie said, knowing he could be trusted. She quickly told him about Gwen, about her cousin's sad predicament and what had led up to it all. "Though maybe, in a way, it's better that she's locked up for a while. Whoever did this can't get to her there."

"Your poor cousin," Father Malone murmured, his expression thoughtful.

"I'm sure she did not do it. There were so many people who hated Mr. Bishop, and I'm having a terrible time sorting it all out. Like a picture puzzle where someone lost the center pieces or something." She glanced around at the busy plaza, the people hurrying around them. Anyone could be listening. "I should love to tell you all about it and hear your opinion."

"And I would love to help in any way I can. I'm sure if we put our heads together, we can find those puzzle pieces again and put them where they belong. Just let me check the parish schedule for the next day or two."

"Oh, wonderful, Father! Phone as soon as you can. I'm going to bake some scones, and I did promise to loan you *The Secrets of Dunstan's Tower*, didn't I?"

They promised to meet up soon to consult, and

Maddie hurried off to buy her ingredients for the scones. She noticed the Ortiz fruit shop was closed and hoped they had gotten Maria off somewhere safe, where she could not get mixed up with the likes of a cad like Bishop again.

As she got closer to her Canyon Road home, the town grew quieter, and she could hear only the faraway shriek of children playing, the squawk of someone's chickens, a dog's bark. She went around to see if Gunther was at home, but his typewriter wasn't on the portal and his shutters were closed. Maddie sighed. She had hoped to get his opinion on Gwen's predicament, too, but it would have to wait.

Disappointed, she went through her garden toward the back door, past the salt cedar tree where the twins climbed. It was much too quiet around the place now that they were at school, but the scent from the last of her roses was heavy and sweet, and helped her feel a bit calmer.

Until she suddenly paused on the gravel pathway. A strange tingling feeling crept along the back of her neck, under the edge of her bobbed hair. As if all was still not quite as it should be. What was amiss? The house looked peaceful enough, some of the windows opened for airing, sheets flapping on the clotheslines.

She glanced toward her studio. The small building, which had once been a garden shed that she had converted to a bright space for her painting, was off-limits to everyone else, much like Juanita with her kitchen. Juanita never cleaned there, and the twins only came inside for sittings when Maddie sketched their portraits. They would never invade that space.

Yet the door was ajar.

Cold trickled down her spine. She tiptoed closer, her breath short, caught between anger and fear. There was no light from beyond the door, but it was definitely open, the lock broken, swaying slightly in the breeze.

"Who is there?" Maddie called, and stood very still to try and hear any hint of sound. There was only the rustling of the trees. No voices, no footsteps, no gunshots.

She carefully eased open the door and peered inside. Dust motes floated in the sunlight from the tall windows. She could see paintings leaning against the walls, smell the sharpness of turpentine and oil paints.

Holding her breath, she stepped inside. The finished paintings in their storage spots were undisturbed, but her easel and the table that held her precious new art supplies just arrived from New York were knocked over. The pastels were broken and ground into the old carpet that covered the stone floor.

And pinned to the smeared canvas she had been working on was a white paper.

Maddie snatched it up and scanned the black, block letters there. Just like the ones in the notes from Luther's office.

Stop poking your nose into things that don't concern you, or you'll be sorry. You don't want to end up like Bishop or your pretty cousin.

Furious, she crumpled it up and tossed it to the floor, then immediately realized she shouldn't have done that. She would have to show it to Inspector Sadler. She shoved it into her jacket pocket and quickly checked to make sure nothing had been taken from the studio. She refused to be afraid of anyone now!

She wouldn't, she couldn't, back down.

CHAPTER 13

Her house was thankfully quiet when Maddie made her way back inside, after making sure the studio had a makeshift lock on the door. Juanita had gone to the shops with the girls. Only Eddie was there, reading in the kitchen while Buttercup snored at his feet under the table. Some watchdog she was.

"Eddie," she asked carefully, not wanting to scare him or make him go running out to catch the thief himself. The boy had a streak of fearless temper in him. "Have you seen anyone else around the house today?"

He shook his head, barely glancing up from the book open in front of him on the kitchen table. "Just Mr. Ryder leaving when I first got home. He waved and drove off in that Duesenberg of his. Do you think he'll ever let me drive it?"

"Not a chance. Was that long ago?"

"Maybe about an hour? That's when I got home from work. It's been quiet since then."

"What are you reading, then?" Maddie asked, as she took a bottle of soda water from the icebox and poured it into two glasses. She handed him one and then took a long sip herself, trying to stay calm. To pretend everything was totally normal.

Eddie held up his book, *The Diners Out Handbook: A Pocket Handbook on the Manners and Customs of Society Functions*.

"Studying up for work?" Maddie asked.

"It's all so interesting," Eddie said. "The right wine with each course, where the napkins go beside the plate, who goes in to dinner first. I never knew all this!"

"Anton will have to watch out for his job."

"Not for a while! But maybe someday. Might be fun." Eddie put down the book as Maddie sat down across from him, sliding a pile of movie mags over to find a place for her glass. "I do like the job, more than I thought I would. People sure are funny when they're staying in a hotel."

"How so?"

"They seem to think they're invisible or something. They leave big messes everywhere, sneak into each other's rooms."

"Shocking!"

Eddie tapped at the movie magazines. "Like that Rex

Neville. All the maids giggle about him, but he seems busy with two ladies already."

Maddie frowned, wondering if these romances had any effect on what happened on the set. "Two?"

"He was up dancing with Lorelei Fontaine until the portal closed, and then he was whispering with Mrs. Bishop in the corner of the lobby."

"He must be awfully energetic."

"June says she thinks he might be getting engaged to Miss Fontaine, though."

"Really? Lorelei?" Maddie thought of how Lorelei and Will were meant to be something of an item. "Why does June think that?"

"She says it's the way they look at each other."

"Hmm. I think maybe *Cinema Romance* said he was almost engaged to Phoebe Torring last year," Maddie said. She flipped through *Romance*'s pages until she found the article. "Not that it means anything. I've heard studios can engineer engagements if they need a bit of publicity."

"Then maybe they're doing that with Neville and Miss Fontaine now?"

"I don't think Lorelei is famous enough for something like that. Unless they're going for a Cinderella story." Maddie looked absently through the magazine—and froze when she noticed one photo. A man in costume as a Victorian lordling, not the youngest but quite handsome, tall and broad-shouldered, with thick dark hair.

Harry Kelly, the caption said. *On the set of his latest, a film version of Dickens'* Bleak House, *eagerly awaited by his fans! He hasn't been seen on the silver screen in too long.*

Mr. Kelly did look vaguely familiar, but from where? Maybe just seeing him in the movies? That would make sense, but somehow Maddie didn't think that was it. It was there, lurking in the back of her mind, but she couldn't quite put it together.

She did recall that Harry Kelly had been tossed off *The Far Sunset* in favor of Rex Neville.

"Eddie, have you seen this man around La Fonda?" she asked, showing him the photo.

"He does look familiar, but I don't think he's a guest there. Maybe he's been in the restaurant?"

"The restaurant? Are you sure?"

Eddie shrugged. "Not really. He just looks like someone I might have seen."

"Me, too."

"June did say she reckons Mrs. Bishop's having a little romance," Eddie said. "What's good for the goose and all that. June saw a man slipping out of her room early in the morning, more than once."

Bridget having a fling, too? Not that Maddie could blame her one bit; in fact, she applauded her for getting a little of her own back after being married to a horror like Luther. But what if she wanted more than a little romance? Maybe wanted to marry again, without losing any money from her first marriage? Or maybe it wasn't even a romance at all, but some sneaky business arrangement to do with the movie? "Does June know who this man was?"

Eddie shook his head. "She says he was wearing a dark dressing gown, tallish, not fat. The lights were dim. But the other maids say it's nothing unusual, those movie people are always in and out of each other's rooms. You'd think they'd be a little more careful about being seen."

"Maybe it has something to do with being far from home," Maddie said musingly. "A holiday mindset."

"You won't tell Ma all this, will you?" Eddie said. "She might not want me to work there anymore. And I can help Señorita Gwen. Keep my ears open, stuff like that."

Maddie was quite alarmed. "I don't want you in harm's way, Eddie, no more than your mother does."

"I know how to be careful." He took another cookie and glanced down at his etiquette book. "Real life really is more interesting than any film out there. Maybe I could write a book about it one day."

Buttercup roused herself from her nap and went to the back door, whining to go out. As Eddie let her out and took his book off to study in the guesthouse, Maddie got out one of her sketchbooks to make notes about any possible suspects. Gwen's life depended on it. She was still scribbling when Juanita came in with her market baskets.

"Señora Maddie, you're back! Shall I make you a snack? I got some things to take Señorita Gwen later, the poor girl," she said, taking off her hat and reaching for her apron. "What are you working on there? Ideas for a new painting?"

"Nothing so fun," Maddie said with a sigh. She decided to wait and tell Juanita about the break-in at the studio later. She didn't want to alarm her, but they all needed to be on their guard. "I was trying to make a list of possible murderers."

"Who do you have so far?" Juanita said as she took ingredients from the cupboards and a box of cookies.

As Juanita sorted out the snacks, Maddie read down her list. "Luther Bishop was not a popular man, so the list is long. But some of them might be a bit far-fetched."

"Sometimes the least likely solution is the right one."

Maddie nodded. That was true enough. "Well, there's Bridget Bishop, of course. They weren't the most—fond couple, were they? And she seems really happy to be in full charge of the film."

"She would seem the most obvious choice, then."

"I would say so, too, but I'm just not sure."

"How come, Señora Maddie?"

Maddie shrugged. "Just a feeling, of course. Bridget doesn't seem sorrowful about her husband, but neither does she seem at all—I don't know. Worried? Guilt-stricken? She might just be a stone-cold psychopath. I *could* see her getting rid of him, if she thought her career was in danger, but how could she have strung Luther up? She's so tiny."

"Someone helped her?"

"Possibly. Okay, she's top of the list."

Juanita started chopping carrots, the steady, soft thwacking sound weirdly soothing. "Who else?"

"Almost anyone working on the picture, I guess. Rex Neville didn't want the part in the first place. Luther must have had something to hold over him to get him to leave that film in Germany." Something like evidence of drug use in a photo. And then there was Phil Ballard and his male lover. Maddie added Phil to the list, but didn't say anything to Juanita. "Lorelei Fontaine wanted to act. Luther promised her a part if she worked on wardrobe, but then he backed out of the deal."

"She has a part now."

"Yes, because Bridget is now in charge and gave it to her. But it's the same problem as with Bridget—how could she physically hang a tall man like Luther?"

"Francisco says the crew didn't like Mr. Bishop, either. Bill Ackerman, the head cameraman, was always cursing him, saying Mr. Bishop didn't know anything about cameras and was always having tantrums when they couldn't do the impossible. Wasted a lot of time, and he and Mr. Ackerman often had—words."

Maddie had seen Bill Ackerman's quick temper and

could imagine what those *words* might have been. Also, there had been some hand-rolled cigarettes in the ashtray outside Luther's office, along with Bridget's Chesterfields and the lipstick-stained glasses. And someone had sabotaged his camera. "So, Bill Ackerman, along with any other crew members."

"What about Mr. Royle?"

Maddie looked up at Juanita in surprise. "Will?"

"I know he's your old friend, and he seems very nice, but maybe he hated working for Mr. Bishop, too? Maybe he wants to write something else. Or maybe they were romantic rivals."

Maddie tapped her pencil on the table as she thought it over. There *was* Lorelei, "friends" with Will, maybe having an affair with Luther, and possibly engaged to Rex Neville. "Maybe, yes. Will does have an artistic sensitivity; his emotions might have gotten the better of him. I think he would be more likely to do something in the heat of the moment, though. A stabbing or maybe a blow to the head rather than drugging and hanging."

"And there is poor Señorita Gwen."

"Yes," Maddie said sadly. "She really hasn't been herself lately, even before the arrest. She's so upset about the whole Luther Bishop thing; he was such a cad to her." She frowned as she remembered Gwen's arrival at the museum, so tearful and agitated. "I think she *could* have killed him, or at least wanted to, but like Will, it's the heat-of-the-moment thing. Is she cool-headed enough to plan the whole thing out?" The impulsive, affectionate, sweet cousin she knew in New York never could have—but maybe movie life had changed her.

"Who else, Señora Maddie?"

Maddie gave a wry laugh. "Besides everyone on the film set, you mean? Maybe Mr. Ortiz? He very well might have been willing to do anything to protect his daughter, and I can't blame him."

"Neither can I," Juanita said with a quiet ferocity, and they nodded together as they thought of the twins. Maddie would certainly do anything to protect their sweetness, their innocent confidence, from some vile predator. But had Mr. Ortiz had the opportunity?

"I guess there are a few people who are not very likely, but who should go on the list," Maddie said. "Alice Henderson was very worried her husband had invested too much on the movie and was set to lose it all. I'm sure there are other investors in the same boat. And who knows how many people in the movie business altogether hated him. He could have been taking mob money, too."

"It's just like life at the pueblo. Everyone is connected, everyone knows each other's business." Juanita slid the chopped vegetables into the pot and reached for a newspaper-wrapped packet. When she opened it, the rich, pungent, earthy aroma of green chilies burst into the air.

"For your lamb stew?" Maddie said.

"Of course, for dinner tomorrow. Since Dr. David is taking you out this evening, isn't he? You should invite him over tomorrow night. We all need a hearty, home-cooked meal." Juanita sliced up the roasted chilies into fine pieces and stirred them into the pot. "So what about that Miss DuLaps? Is she tied in with Mr. Bishop's death, too?"

"Her livelihood is gossip, true, but would she kill someone to create a story?" Maddie wouldn't put it past her. Anyone who could purposely buy those hats couldn't be entirely sane.

"And they say Mr. Bishop was involved with drugs. It could be a fight over all that nasty business."

"Possibly. Maybe. I don't know." Maddie rubbed at her aching temples. "David can tell us more about exactly when and how Luther died once he finishes the autopsy."

"You know, Señora Maddie, maybe you should talk to Dr. Cole about something else. Something pleasant! It would make you both happier," Juanita said. She took the chunks of lamb for the stew from the icebox and thwacked them hard with a cleaver. "Francisco says the women in Hollywood are so hard, always talking work, work, work, and it's impossible for romance to bloom."

Maddie laughed. "Oh, your Francisco says, does he? Is he behind this sudden concern with romance?"

Juanita's cheeks turned pink, and she took another hard swing of the cleaver. "We just like to talk about old times. But he's right. Dr. Cole is a nice man, and he works too hard, as do you, Señora Maddie. You both deserve a little rest sometimes."

Maddie remembered David's kiss, and ducked her head to hide her own blush. She hadn't been thinking about anything else at all in that moment when he took her in his arms. "That would be nice, I admit. But first, we have to get Gwen out of Inspector Sadler's beady little sites. After the murderer is caught and the movie leaves town, things will quiet down again. Or will you be too sad, because the handsome Francisco will leave, too?"

"You're teasing me, Señora Maddie."

Maddie laughed. "Maybe just a little. I don't get to do that nearly often enough." She showed Juanita the movie mag photo of Harry Kelly. "Do you think you've seen this man around here lately?"

Juanita frowned as she studied it. "I don't know. He's very handsome, I'm sure I would remember him. Is he with the movie, too?"

Maddie sighed. "I don't know. Oh, Juanita, I just don't seem to know anything any longer."

CHAPTER 14

After an hour, Maddie left Juanita to fix supper and went back to the studio for a while. She had to clean up, and she refused to let anyone scare her away from her own work! If they came back, she would be ready for them. Besides, she hadn't been working for a while, not since the movie business came to take up everyone's time and thoughts, and she itched with missing it.

She pushed away the bad day, Gwen in jail and threatening notes, and took out her current work in progress, a scene of the mountains and a river much like the set, and gave it a fresh look. Maybe if she turned her mind to something besides the suspects, a new idea would occur to her. As she worked, time flew past, as it always did, and the light lengthened at the windows.

A knock at the studio door surprised her, and she glanced up at the clock on the shelf to see that a couple of hours had already gone by. She wiped her paint-splattered hands on her smock and hurried to answer the door.

David stood there, impossibly handsome with the late afternoon sunlight turning his hair to molten gold, his eyes the piercing pale blue of the sky itself. He smiled and held out a box of her favorite caramel cream chocolates. "Juanita said you were out here. Am I interrupting? I can come back later . . ."

"Not at all! Come in." Maddie stood back to let him through the door. It was actually the first time he had ever been in her studio; she didn't usually let anyone inside. She popped one of the chocolates into her mouth as he studied the art on the wall, stacked along the floor, and she wondered achingly what he might think.

"That's just some early stuff," she said when he stopped at a scene of her own garden, an experiment on trying to capture the shadows as they moved beneath the trees. It had never been finished. "I hadn't quite figured out how to make it look right. I still haven't."

"I love it," he answered, still staring at the scene. "The contrast between the bright sun through the clouds here, the shadows lengthening. It's marvelous."

Maddie felt her cheeks turn warm, and she wanted to grin like a schoolgirl. "Do you think so?" She wondered if she should finish it and give it to him for his birthday.

When *was* his birthday? There were so many things she didn't yet know about him.

"I do." He turned to her with a smile. "I came to see if I could tempt you out to dinner. Juanita said you had a long day at the movie set."

"Oh, I'd like that. If it's someplace informal. I feel a bit of a mess."

His smile widened, and he took her into his arms. "I think you look gorgeous, as always. I'm surprised they haven't recruited you to star in the film yet."

Maddie laughed. "Flattery will get you everywhere, doctor." She went up on tiptoe to kiss him, and it was so sweet and delightful and fun that even more time slipped past before she could even notice.

All too soon, she had to go to the house and get cleaned up to go out to dinner. She had to drag David away from Juanita plying him with biscochitos and the twins showing him their homework, but at last they agreed Maddie could leave. She gathered up her gloves and handbag and took David's arm as he led her from the house and down the quiet street into the evening.

"How have your days been on the glamorous movie set, then?" he asked as they strolled down the walkway. "No more gruesome deaths, I hope."

Maddie decided not to tell him about the note in the studio, not until she had worked some clues out for herself first. He had enough to worry about at work. "Not yet. Things seem a bit chaotic, though, as Bridget takes charge. She seems to do a better job than her husband, I must say. She has such an enviable energy."

"Maybe she just wanted the movie to herself, then, and did away with the philandering Mr. Bishop."

Maddie sighed. "It sounds silly, doesn't it? But they don't seem like normal-thinking people at all. The movie, their ambition, it's everything to them. I honestly wouldn't be surprised if *any* of them had decided Luther Bishop was standing in the way of their career and had to go. And I admit, if I found myself married to the man, I might be tempted to strychnine up his coffee a little. Such a bully."

David laughed as he held open the door to the little, noisy café tucked away on the winding Burro Alley. "Remind me to always mind all my p's and q's with you, Maddie."

She laughed, too, and dropped gratefully into the cracked leather booth. She hadn't realized how tired being on the set all day, not to mention studying each face she saw with deep suspicion and her mind racing with thoughts of their motives and opportunities, made her feel. She felt bone-deep weary. "Not you, darling. You are much too sweet and charming, not to mention handsome. I would never use something so painful as strychnine. Besides, it's so useful to have doctor on call."

"Glad I can be of use, then." He studied the menu and

Maddie studied him, the lovely angles of his face with its blade-sharp nose and high cheekbones, the square chin set off with his gold-and-silver short-trimmed beard, the glow of those eyes. She remembered what he'd said about his wife, the deep sadness she'd seen in those same eyes as he recalled the agony of it all, and her heart ached for him. The world was so full of sadness, loss, and pain, so much of which couldn't be avoided. Why would anyone want to create death and destruction?

"Would it have been painful?" she asked. "For Luther Bishop, I mean."

David frowned in thought. "He had enough morphine in him to knock over a horse. I doubt he knew a thing."

Maddie shivered. "Poor man. He might not have been very nice, but surely no one deserves that. Could it maybe have been an accident?"

"He took so much of the drug, he didn't know what he was doing?"

"Yes. I know booze is more the thing around here . . ."

"But he's a big Hollywood producer."

"Surely he could get whatever he wanted in the way of illegal substances?" She paused when the waitress came to pour out welcome cups of strong coffee and take their order. "You know Elizabeth Grover?"

"She comes to the surgery once in a while, stomach complaints mostly."

"Well, I know she gets cocaine sometimes. Surely her supplier could have worked for Luther, too."

"All the comforts of California in the desert."

Maddie sighed and took a deep gulp of the strong, blessedly fortifying coffee. "The world does get smaller and smaller."

"I've seen stranger things happen to people under the influence of substances, but I doubt Bishop could have moved at all with such an amount in his system. I think he would have been barely alive, if at all, when he was hanged."

"So someone else would have had to string him up?"

"Probably to make it look like suicide, or as you thought, maybe an accident while under the influence."

"It would surely have to be someone strong, then." Not someone like Gwen, or Bridget Bishop, or even Evie DuLaps.

"I would certainly imagine so." The waitress brought out their food, lovely steaming platters, and he smiled down at it like a drowning man with a life preserver. Maddie suddenly wished she *were* a cook and could feed him up after long hours at the hospital. A painting would just have to do. "Do you know if he was already an addict? Needing more and more to get a fix?"

Maddie shrugged as she buttered a roll. "Possibly. I hear gossip about all sorts of things on movie sets. Long hours, irregular sleep, they all seem to need a bit of help.

But Luther Bishop seemed *too* energetic. I'm not sure morphine would be his choice."

"He certainly didn't appear to be a habitual user, and there were no other drugs in his system," David said. "In fact, he was remarkably healthy. Strong heart and lungs. It's sad." He took a hearty bite of his steak and gave her a rueful smile. "Sorry, this hardly seems like good dinner table conversation. My mother always got so mad at my father for 'talking shop' over the roast."

Maddie laughed. "I don't mind. I have a strong enough stomach. But I guess I wouldn't mind talking about something more cheerful, too."

As they finished their meal, they talked more about art, the local painters in town, plans for the next museum show, Maddie's new projects, and then some of David's funnier patients at the hospital, including Mrs. Garcia, the elderly housekeeper to the Hendersons, who liked to say loudly about her ailments, "Lawks, it's just my glands!"

But then that made Maddie wonder about the Hendersons and the money they were losing on the film, and if anyone else was worried about their investment. Worried enough to do something about it? Money was a very powerful motive. She sighed, sure she never would get away from the dratted movie.

After dinner, she happily leaned against David as they walked home, staring up at the sliver of moon just appearing above one of the square stone towers of the cathedral.

The stained-glass windows shimmered in the encroaching night. She thought of evenings she had once spent in New York with Gwen, with a different sky above them, different music. Hopes and dreams, both of them so young.

"How very fast time goes," she mused. "One second you're out walking with Nanny, pushing a doll pram, thinking you'll *never* get to be grown up, and then—it's all far behind you. All been had already."

David glanced down at her, his expression surprised. "I seriously doubt all your happiness has already been had, Maddie. At least, I hope it hasn't. But I definitely know that melancholy feeling. Have your cousin and your old friend Mr. Royle being here made you feel homesick?"

"Not homesick, exactly. I know I belong here now, not in New York, and not with my family. After Pete died, I just couldn't do what they expected, follow the old ways. The world isn't like that anymore, even if we might wish it could be. But I guess Gwen and Will do make me feel a little—wistful. When I was a girl, I felt safe. Now nowhere is safe, really. So I wonder what it would be like if I was still tucked away in my childhood room." The cathedral bells tolled the hour, slow and deep and sonorous, comforting. A spot of something seemingly permanent in a shifting world. "Do you ever miss England?"

"Things about it, I guess. Good fish and chips, definitely," he said vaguely.

Maddie smiled, yet she wished he wouldn't be so elusive, his confidences so fleeting and precious. He wasn't like Will, so open and confiding.

They turned a corner, and Maddie noticed that Mr. Ortiz's shop was still closed up and dark. Not so strange after business hours, of course, but even the windows upstairs, where the family lived, were shuttered and quiet. She wondered if they really had taken Maria away to get over what had happened. The poor girl.

"I know what might distract us from such down-in-the-dumps memories," David said.

Maddie laughed, and impulsively turned to wrap her arms around him. He did feel so yummy, so strong and warm. "A spot of canoodling? Doctor, how shocking!"

He laughed, too, and held her close. "Well, that as well. Afterwards. Do you have time to stop at the hospital?"

"Where there are all those empty rooms? I declare, doctor, but you *are* a cad."

His laughter grew louder, and he took her hand to tug her down the street. "Oh, just come on!"

They hurried, still giggling just a bit, toward the hospital. The corridors were shadowed, only about half the lamps lit, and everything was quiet except for a few murmurs from some of the patients' rooms. Maddie could hear the soft patter of nurses' feet, but she didn't see anyone. She remembered stories of spirits wandering the floors at night, whispering in the basement, and she felt a nervous flutter deep inside, yet David's hand on hers held her steady. And she was much too curious to turn back now.

She followed him down a flight of stairs and through some metal doors into a kitchen. It was vast and industrial, all shining chrome and white enamel, the tiled floor gleamingly clean, the stacks of clean dishes behind the glass cupboard doors perfectly aligned. It smelled of bleach and baked potatoes.

"What are we doing?" she whispered.

"I'm just curious about something," David said. He opened one of the walk-in pantries and scanned the shelves of flour, tubs of salt, jars of dried fruit. "How much would you say Luther Bishop weighed? 200, 220?"

"I'm not sure. 200, maybe? He was tall but lean. Must have burned off energy yelling at everyone on set."

"I think you're right." David disappeared into the darkened closet and came out with two large bags of onions and a length of rope. "Here, help me find a stool."

"Oh, I see!" Maddie cried. "The onions are Luther?"

"Yes. Let's see if one person, say myself or even you, could string him up alone."

Maddie found a stool near the iceboxes and set it up under a network of heating pipes crisscrossing the ceiling. She watched as David tied a noose from the rope and looped the loose end over the pipes, tightening it until it held steady and a long length of it fell to the floor. He put the noose around the bags of onions and tested it to make sure it would hold. "Give it a try."

She took hold of the end of the rope and yanked it with all her strength, bracing her heeled shoes on the tiles. It raised a bit, but then dropped again with a thud.

"I don't think I could have hoisted him up that high," she gasped.

"No, I can see that. Nor could you have tied him steady so he would hang there. But he did drop more than he should have without breaking his neck." David took the rope from her and pulled back. He got the onions up much higher, and then the rope slid through his hands. He tied it off, and they stared at the bag swaying horribly at the end of the rope. Maddie felt quite nauseous.

"Probably not a woman, then," she said. All the ladies on the set were fashionably slight.

"Maybe not alone," David said thoughtfully, rubbing at his chin as he studied the rope, the stool, the weight. "But with some help, possibly. Everyone we know disliked our Mr. Bishop, didn't they?"

"Who knows how many people could have been in on it," Maddie said with a sigh. And if people were working together on the murder, who could have paired off? Bridget and an unknown lover? Maybe Lorelei, with Rex or even Will? Someone else, someone with a grudge against Luther who hadn't even revealed themselves yet? He had blackmailed and bullied so many.

"Oh, my poor Gwen," she whispered.

★   ★   ★

That night, Maddie couldn't fall asleep. She kept tossing in her bed, tangling up the blankets. Thoughts kept running through her mind, images of Luther Bishop and his death, Gwen in the jail, the movie set, the note in her studio. And the glow of the nearly full moon through her thin muslin curtains didn't help.

Finally, she just gave up and reached for her dressing gown. If she couldn't sleep anyway, she would just make some cocoa and let herself worry. Maybe she could turn her thoughts in a different direction, see the problems in a way she hadn't before.

As she waited for the water to boil in the kitchen, she pushed open the back door to the garden and studied the moonlit scene. Her studio was dark and quiet, safely locked again, her flowers, usually all red and pink and yellow, turned silver in the night. Juanita's guesthouse at the back of the garden was dark, Buttercup sleeping on the doorstep. The dog liked to move around at night, sleeping on Maddie's bed, with the twins, in the garden or the pantry as the mood took her. A free spirit, like Maddie herself. The thought made her smile, and she called softly to Buttercup.

She knelt down to scratch the dog's ears and caught a glimpse of a flash of light from Gunther's house as his door opened onto his portal.

In that instant of light, she saw Gunther with another person, their arms around each other. The man was quite tall, broad-shouldered, his hair a blur of salt and pepper in the shadows.

Phil Ballard. They kissed and held on tightly to each other for a long moment before Phil slipped away and was lost in the night. After a minute, she heard the purr of a car motor taking off into the distance. Gunther lingered on the portal, and Maddie saw the flare of his cigarette lighter, the tiny red glow.

She froze, not wanting to embarrass her friend, but she couldn't hide the reflection of her pale-pink dressing gown.

"Maddie," Gunther called softly. "You're up late."

She stood up and went to the fence between their gardens, Buttercup at her heels. "So are you," she said. "I wasn't spying, Gunther, I swear."

Gunther gave a sigh. "I know you weren't, my darling. And I know that you understand that feeling when we must snatch a bit of forgetfulness wherever we find it."

"Is that all it is?" she asked gently. "A bit of forgetfulness?"

"Of course, dearest. What else could it be? He is in California, a famous movie star, and I am here, and never the twain shall meet. Romances like mine can't be anything but fleeting, I fear. But he is lovely, don't you think? My own film idol, for a little while anyway."

Maddie thought of her studio being broken into, and the incriminating photos in Luther Ballard's box. She wanted to warn Gunther, but how could she now? How could she mar his moment of happiness, bittersweet as it was? "Gunther, dear, I do think—I wonder . . ."

"Oh, I know, Maddie. We don't know who killed the appalling Mr. Bishop yet; it could be anyone. And Phil hated the man."

"Rightfully so," Maddie said. "Bishop was a bully and a blackmailer. I'm sure Mr. Ballard would have been utterly justified."

Gunther took a long drag on his cigarette. "And he is so very good at playing the villain in his movies."

"He is." Maddie remembered the menacing aura of him as he stalked Bridget in their film scene—and the man's gentleness and humor in real life. His fear and shame over those photos. "I just worry about everyone these days, Gunther darling. I don't want anyone else I care about to end up like Gwen."

"Don't worry, my love. I'm a tough old bird; you know that." They stood together in the night for a long, quiet moment, wreathed in silvery smoke. "But the worry *is* mutual. I hope you are taking care of yourself."

"Of course I am."

Gunther shook his head. "Remember what happened last time? You put yourself in danger without a thought, dearest, to help anyone who needs it. Just be very careful. For me?"

"I'm always careful!"

He reached out and squeezed her hand. "I couldn't bear to lose you, too. Let's have dinner at La Fonda tomorrow, yes? Bring your gorgeous doctor. We could all use a little forgetfulness."

Without another word, he turned and went back into his house, shutting the door. Maddie returned to her kitchen and mixed up some cocoa, wishing she could close out the real world just as easily as that.

CHAPTER 15

It was a beautiful night as Maddie walked with David to La Fonda, the stars blinking on in the dusky-blue sky like tiny diamonds. The chilly, sparkling clarity of it all made her feel at the same time a pang of melancholy and so happy she could burst from it all. She often felt that way in New Mexico, so intensely alive, as if she stood perched on the verge of something immense and beyond understanding.

Yet with the terrible business lately, that sharp, sudden reminder of the fragility of everything, and with Gwen making her think of her family and their old life in New York, it all felt—closer. Darker. More immediate. Like a gray cloud had descended from the bright blue sky, threatening to engulf her as it had after Pete died.

She sighed, and leaned on David's shoulder as they strolled past the Loretto Chapel of the Sisters, its elegant spire twisting up toward the stars. A light glowed in the rose window, jeweled red and blue and gold. The sight was so gorgeous she felt warm and steady, and David smelled so delicious next to her, solid and real and good. Yet he seemed quiet tonight, too, far away, almost sad.

"You're very quiet tonight, Maddie," he said with a small smile. "Pence for your thoughts?"

She laughed. "You and your English money! How much is that worth?"

"Oh, a few cents."

"Well, I will give them to you for free. If you really want them."

"I always want to hear your thoughts. Maybe you're still worried about what happened to Luther Bishop? Anyone would be."

"Of course I am. I can't remember anything so scandalous since I've been here. And with poor Gwen right in the middle of it all . . ."

David's steps slowed, and he leaned back on the low wall that marked off the chapel property from La Fonda. His face was solemn and shadowed in the streetlights. "I'm afraid it really looks like he didn't kill himself. The toxicology reports came back. He had enough morphine in his system to knock out a horse, plus a good quantity of whiskey. It would have been hard for him to stand, let alone string himself up, as we saw ourselves with our little experiment."

"Yes, of course." Maddie paused to think of everyone on the movie set who had reason to dislike Bishop, including Gwen. Suddenly unable to stand, her knees trembling, she sat down hard on the adobe wall next to David. He jumped up beside her, his arm steady around her. He was always so calm, so strong, always helping everyone else. She wondered how he stayed so steady, after all he had seen, both in the war and in his hospital work. She feared she couldn't do without him, and it scared her to think of losing him as she had Pete.

"Have you talked to the police?" she asked.

"Inspector Sadler is coming to the hospital tomorrow. I doubt the results will surprise him any more than they have us. I'm sure Mrs. Bishop will want to make her arrangements, though."

Maddie nodded. They sat in silence for several long minutes, watching the stars flash and glimmer overhead. She thought about Gwen and how it had been when they were girls and would hide away in the attic to tell their secrets, their dreams. They could never have foreseen this. All of them had been tossed around by the world, by love and loss and the way the whole universe had been upended by war and epidemic.

She had come to Santa Fe for the beauty and simplicity of it, the mountains and the endless desert, the sky, the silence, the feeling of being so distant from everything. From being so small, yet part of something beyond understanding. Fleeing everything that had hurt her and made her feel alone.

But in truth, nothing was ever simple. Nothing was distant. All things were connected.

"Do you ever think about when you were young, back in Brighton?" she asked. "Do you ever wish you could go back to that, when everything seemed—certain? When you knew there was a place you belonged?"

He was silent for a long moment, and she glanced at him. In the faint light from the chapel windows, he looked as if he was carved of marble, still and quiet and serious. He shook his head. "I'm not sure I ever felt there was a place I belonged. My father was busy with his medical practice, my mother was very involved in suffragette work, and I had no siblings. Home was quiet, and I changed schools rather a lot. Sometimes I would even go to live with my grandparents in London, where my grandfather had his own medical office. But I know what you mean. When we're young, we know what's expected of us. What the consequences of our actions will be. Have you been missing New York since your cousin arrived?"

"Not exactly." Maddie studied the chapel's spire, but in her mind she saw something else, a busy street, hurrying people, pale mansions with every window lit. "New York is nothing like here, of course. There are so many people there, so many things happening at every moment, so many people watching. I can breathe here. I can paint.

I can be free in a way I never could before. But I guess I've been thinking about my family, and how it was when I was a girl. There was such a rhythm to things. I thought I understood people then, including myself. Now I see I don't understand anything at all."

He nodded. "I knew after the war I couldn't go back to Brighton. It would be impossible for me just to slip into working at my father's clinic, as he always wanted me to. To have a life just like his. Nothing felt the same anymore."

"And then your wife died, too?"

"Yes." He went quiet, his gaze very distant. "She didn't actually die in the flu epidemic before I could see her again after the war. That was what her family wanted to be said, and I would have done anything to ease their pain a bit."

Maddie was confused. He had never spoken much about his wife, just that they had been young newlyweds when he went to battle, that she died of the flu. "What do you mean?"

"She killed herself. An overdose of morphine." He looked down at Maddie, and she could read nothing in his beautiful blue eyes. Nothing but an old, bruised pain she recognized too well. The pain of a loss that could never be recovered or soothed. "We had a hard time after being apart so long, and we separated right after I came home. I lived in London while she stayed in Brighton, but I was sure that with a bit of time we would be fine. After she died, though, it was found she was pregnant—by her lover."

"Oh, David," Maddie whispered in horror. "Oh, no." She gently touched his arm, wishing with all her might she knew how to comfort him. Make the past better. But she knew she never could. "I am so sorry. All this Bishop business must be bringing up some terrible memories."

"It's not the same, I know. But I couldn't help her either, just as I can't really help now. It's a terrible feeling, this helplessness."

"I think . . ."

"Maddie, darling! Whatever are you doing sitting about out here when the party is next door?"

Maddie quickly wiped at her eyes at the sound of her name, and turned to see Gunther making his way down the empty street toward them. He was smiling and waving merrily, the bittersweet moment of last night hidden.

"We just stopped for a . . . well," Maddie said weakly. She looked up at David and saw he was trying to smile now, too.

"A wee little smooch, I bet," Gunther said. "Don't worry, my dears, your secret is safe with me."

The three of them made their way across the street and through the heavy, carved doors into the lobby. It was already very busy, the light and noise a sharp contrast to the piercing, starlit silence outside. Anton, the hotel's dashing, hospitable manager, greeted them, and told them the others were gathering on the back portal.

"You go on ahead," Maddie told David and Gunther as she handed the cloakroom attendant her velvet jacket. "I'm just going to freshen up a bit."

The ladies' powder room was past the lifts on a back corridor lined with quiet rooms. Maddie had been there on the night Tomas Anaya was murdered, had stood on the same spot on the red-and-blue Navajo rug when the body was carried past. She felt sick to remember it. But at least then the killer had been caught.

She remembered some of the people she had met while looking into Tomas's death, the tangle of illicit business dealings and illegal operations that went on everywhere, even in quiet Santa Fe. She'd heard that gangsters also liked the movie business, its labyrinthinc system of theaters, distribution deals, and contracts ripe for easy skimming. Everyone had said *The Far Sunset* was an expensive picture, but Luther was determined to make it. Maybe he'd had dealings with criminal elements and they were tired of the delays? It would make sense, and Maddie would love it if no one she knew had been involved in his death, but she didn't know how to even begin to find out. Maybe she could ask Tomas's cousin Mavis, who used to work in a brothel just outside town and now waited tables at a café near the train station. She knew all sorts of types.

Maddie sighed. What hashes people made of their

lives, she thought sadly. One mistake, and it was too easy to tumble down the mountain. And almost impossible to get up again.

Maddie spun around and pushed open the door to the ladies' room. She was startled to find she wasn't alone. Elizabeth Grover stood in front of the hammered tin–framed mirror, her beaded handbag open on the counter.

For an instant, Maddie was sure she really had tumbled back in time to the terrible night Tomas died. Elizabeth had been in the ladies' room then, too, with a bump of cocaine. Tonight she seemed sober enough, if a little distracted. Her steel-gray and lavender chiffon frock made her pale looks even whiter, and she bit her lip as if confused to find herself there.

Maddie remembered Elizabeth had been with some of the movie people when she'd last seen her at lunch in La Fonda's restaurant, and wondered how well Elizabeth knew them. Maybe she had been one of Luther's conquests?

"Hello, Elizabeth," she said. "Feeling okay?"

Elizabeth blinked hard, as if startled, and gave her a bright smile. "Hi, Maddie. Just ducky, thanks. Isn't all this movie business exciting? And now a scandalous death, too. I might as well have never left Buffalo. The shocking gossip of it all!"

Maddie nodded. She knew Elizabeth had come from

back East, too, had some kind of family money, but she didn't know what her story was exactly. A lot of people came to New Mexico to get away from all that, and no one was too nosy. Usually. "Did you know any of them? The movie people, that is?" Maddie asked as she dug her compact out of her bag.

"Oh, I met the Bishops at a party once, back in New York," Elizabeth said. "Bridget was the really famous one back then; she'd just been in that film version of *Macbeth*. So spooky. Even my parents thought she was respectable, being from the legit theater and all. But Luther had ambition, you could see it even then, and real fire to get ahead. A girl can always tell. That poor guy. Who would have thought it would end like this?"

"Yes," Maddie murmured. "Who would have thought. Did you like him, then?"

Elizabeth gave a hoarse laugh. "I've been a fool for plenty of bad men, but not that one. Too blatant even for me. I admit I wouldn't mind trying my hand at the movies, though. Could be fun." She took out a gold tube of lipstick and uncapped it. It looked familiar.

"That's a nice shade," Maddie said.

"Mmm," Elizabeth murmured as she carefully outlined her fashionably bee-stung lips. "Ravishing Rose. It's all the rage now. My sister sent me a whole case."

"I must be behind the fashion times." Maddie

studied her own enameled lipstick tube of plain red, and remembered the stains on the glass outside Luther's office. "Did you ever ask Luther for a part in *The Far Sunset*?"

Elizabeth shook her head. "There are lots more directors out there, and even some who wouldn't give you the hassle Luther would. I'm too busy right now. Besides, Bridget Bishop is the real power in that outfit, mark my words."

Maddie thought of how efficiently Bridget seemed to have taken over the film set. "How so?"

Elizabeth frowned at Maddie in the mirror. "Wanting to be in the movies yourself, Maddie? I heard your painting was going well, after that museum show."

Maddie shrugged. "Nothing creative is ever wasted."

Elizabeth smiled and dropped her lipstick back into her handbag. "And us girls always have to be extra creative to get what we want out of life, don't we?"

"I guess we do."

Elizabeth gave her a twinkling wave and rushed out of the room, leaving a trace of her perfume behind. Not Jicky, Maddie thought. Joy, maybe, sweet and flowery.

Maddie put on a slick of her own lipstick and left the ladies' room. In the hallway outside, a few waiters were rushing past with room service trays, and one of them was Eddie.

"Señora Maddie," he said with a grin. "Come for the party out on the portal?"

"Indeed I have, and you look very professional tonight, Eddie," she answered, and he really did. He seemed to be growing up faster every minute, no longer the gangling kid from when she first arrived, but tall, dark-haired, almost dignified in his crisp white shirt. "How's the job going?"

"I like it. Not too hard, and the tips are pretty good." He lowered his voice to whisper, "Are you here looking into the murder? For your cousin, I mean? I can help you out, like I said before."

"Oh, Eddie, no," she said, worried. "Juanita would be so mad if I put you in any danger."

"It'd be easy! All the movie people are staying here, and they just leave stuff all over their rooms."

"Ed! Come on, we have a lot more deliveries to make," one of the other boys called.

Eddie gave her one more grin and hurried away, his tray balanced on his shoulder. "Just think about it, Señora Maddie!"

Maddie knew what she would think about it—she would worry about Eddie getting caught snooping around. She shook her head, wondering how on earth she could discourage him, and turned the corner back toward the lobby. She noticed a woman unlocking the door of one of the guest rooms near the lifts. It was Lorelei, dressed in a gorgeous artistic gown of burgundy-and-green flowered velvet, but she looked tired. Maddie would have thought she'd have been a little more peppy, having gotten a role in the movie as she had wanted.

"Hello, Lorelei," she said.

Lorelei glanced up, her expression startled before she smiled. "Hello, Maddie. Going to the party?"

"Of course. Are you leaving it? Surely it's all just starting."

"I had a tiny headache, just came to fetch a powder. Want to come in for a minute?" Her smile widened, and she added quietly, "I might have some rather nice French champagne hidden in here somewhere, just waiting to be shared."

Maddie wondered if she had imagined that Lorelei looked weary just then, for now she looked positively happy. "I'd never say no to champagne!"

Lorelei led her inside to a small room. It looked as if a tornado had swept through, with gowns and shoes heaped everywhere, papers and sketchbooks piled in a small desk in the corner, lipsticks and powder pots scattered on the dresser. The bed was unmade, heaped with pillows. The embroidered Spanish silk curtains were drawn over the windows, casting it into shadows.

Lorelei took out a bottle from one of the trunks and popped it open with a delightful fizz. It frothed out into tooth glasses from the powder room as she poured. "See, the real stuff, from France. Can't be beat."

"No, indeed." Maddie took a sip and watched as

Lorelei mixed up a packet of Stop-Ake. "I guess the movie mags like to give the impression you movie people drink this all the time. They say Gloria Swanson even bathes in it!"

Lorelei laughed. "That would be awfully sticky, wouldn't it?" She drained her glass and refilled it. "It's bathtub gin most of the time, if we're lucky. The pay's not bad, but most of us aren't exactly bringing in Pickford-style checks. Not that *she* spends her money on French champagne. Working too hard to get into trouble."

Maddie nodded, thinking of the constant bustle of the movie set. "You all seem to work very hard."

"That's true. Long hours, lots of hurry-up-and-wait, lots of redoing what you just spent a day doing. But it's always interesting work."

"Have you always been in theater?"

Lorelei shook her head. "I started out in straight fashion, working in the cutting room at Saks. I got an apprenticeship at Galeries Lafayette in Paris when I was just sixteen, before the war."

"Paris," Maddie sighed. "How scrumptious."

Lorelei gave a blissful smile, her gaze very faraway. "Oh, it was. I've never loved anything more. The cafés on the Champs-Élysées, the parks, the paintings in the Louvre. And the clothes! I had never seen such things—thick satin, real silk ribbons on lingerie, mink-trimmed coats, the hats."

"So what happened?"

Lorelei grinned and drained her glass. "What happened to all of us, the war. It was terrible, but also kind of great. Such purpose. Such living of life every minute. I started making uniforms and did some nursing. It's how I met Luther Bishop."

Maddie was surprised. She hadn't realized Lorelei had known Luther years before getting into films. "He was a soldier?"

Lorelei laughed. "Him? Of course not. He was making movies. News reels. They came to the hospital where I was working to make one, and I was asked to be one of the 'angels of mercy' in our uniforms, holding patients' hands and looking saintly. It felt silly at first, but then I rather liked it. The patients did, too. Pretending we were someone else for a while. That what was happening around us wasn't real."

Maddie nodded. She remembered that feeling very well when she'd done some volunteer work in the hospital after Pete died, when the boys were coming back from France. It had felt good. For just a moment, she wondered if maybe Lorelei had even met Pete, if she found the old news reels maybe she could glimpse him. But Pete hadn't been in a hospital; he'd died instantly, no pain, according to the letter his commanding officer wrote. She thought of David's wife, the terrible story he had told her, and how the poor woman must have suffered. The pain in David's beautiful blue eyes. There was always enough of that to go around.

She glanced down into the golden depths of her champagne. "That must be nice. Being someone else for a while."

"Yes. I realized I loved it."

"So that's how you got into movie work? Knowing Luther Bishop?"

"Not at all. After the war, I came back to America, got a job at Bendel's in New York. One day I saw an ad in the *Times* calling for wardrobe assistants at a studio out in Jersey. I ended up on a project with Bridget and Luther then."

"Will says you'd like to act as well as work on wardrobe."

"Sure, who wouldn't? I like clothes, to be sure, but I still think about how it to felt to act, to be someone else. When I met Will, he thought I could do it, and he has a good eye. He could be a theater impresario as well as a writer, if he wanted."

"He's always been so creative. Even when we were kids, he would scribble poems all the time. Have the two of you been together long?" Maddie thought of the rumors that Lorelei was involved with Rex.

Lorelei shook her head with a wry smile. "I wouldn't say we're *together* together. He's nice, though. Not like other guys. He certainly listens to girls, hears what they have to say. That's really rare, especially in a man who's such a looker."

"Yes," Maddie murmured, thinking of men like her father and brother, the few suitors she had before Pete, who would talk over a woman for hours. Pete and David weren't like that, though, and neither was Will. "And Bridget is making changes to the story, adding a character for you."

"Yes," Lorelei said jubilantly. "And I'm sure that's thanks to Will. It's going to be a much better picture now that Bridget is in charge." She finished the last drops of her champagne and turned to the dressing table to fix her lipstick. Not Ravishing Rose, Maddie noticed, but a deep, dark vampy red. "Shall we find the party? I bet I've talked your ear right off."

"Not at all. I love people's stories," Maddie said. And she had heard a lot of them lately, the sordid affairs of movie people.

Lorelei tossed a fringed, embroidered flamenco shawl over her velvet dress with a stylish flair Maddie wished she could imitate. She smoothed the skirt of her own Nile-green silk dress, wishing it was a little more— unconventional. She finished her own drink and followed Lorelei out of the room.

The party under the covered portal was already in full swing when they arrived. A phonograph played dance music as couples swept across the tiled floor, moving in and out of the moonlight that peeked through the tall windows to the dark courtyard beyond. Waiters passed around trays of hors d'oeuvres and glasses.

Rex Neville came up to Lorelei as soon they stepped into the room. He looked devastatingly handsome in his dinner jacket, but his expression was strained as he grabbed her arm. "I've been waiting for you, Lorelei," he said quietly. "We need to talk. Dance?"

Lorelei stared up at him for a long moment, a tiny frown on her dark-red lips. Finally, she nodded, and he took her into his arms to sweep her into the steps. They looked as if they were in a movie together already, their heads together as they whispered, their arms tight around each other. Maddie wondered if Lorelei was telling the truth when she said she and Will were not an "item." Maybe she really was romancing Rex Neville instead. If so, she would be the envy of half the women in America.

Maddie looked around for David and saw him at a table near the fireplace talking to Bridget Bishop and Phil Ballard. Bridget was waving her ivory cigarette holder, which matched her creamy silk gown trimmed with black ribbons and gauzy gray roses, as she told them some story. David waved at Maddie, and she waved back and started toward them. But she stopped when Will called her name.

He stood by one of the windows, the courtyard dark beyond the glass, chatting with Gunther. "Maddie,

Gunther here was telling me about this new book he's working on. A romance between an Indian princess and a rancher. It would be the perfect treatment for a movie. So tragic and dramatic, full of sweep."

"Oh, I don't think so," Gunther said, and for the first time since Maddie had known him he actually looked rather bashful. And also hopeful. "I've barely started it." They talked a bit more about stories that did well on film, until Phil Ballard came up, and he and Gunther went for a smoke and a chat near the windows.

"Shall we dance, then, Mads?" Will asked with one of his charming New York smiles. "Show them what we learned back in cotillion?"

Maddie laughed. "That was a million years ago! I'd be a terrible disappointment to Mrs. Granville's lessons now. But I would love to dance."

Will took her hand and spun her in a wide circle, making her laugh even more. They moved into a smooth foxtrot, and for a moment it really *was* as if the years had melted away and they were young again in the marble ballroom above Fifth Avenue. Moving around Mrs. Granville's sprung floor in their white gloves.

"I'm surprised I even remember these steps," Maddie said.

"It's my excellent partnering skills," Will answered, holding his head high as he pretended to preen. "Old Granville did say dancing skills would be useful our whole lives, and she wasn't wrong. Remember when we would sneak away from the deb balls to listen to ragtime in the Village, and twirled around all night long?"

"Of course I do. It was all so marvelous." She smiled wistfully as she remembered that glorious music, the beat so deep it made it feel like the whole world was shifting under her feet. Spinning around and around with Pete and their friends, laughing so much. How angry her mother had been when she stumbled home in the wee hours, and how the little rebellion had just made it that much sweeter. "David and I were just talking about New York. He wanted to know if I miss that life, miss our old world."

"And do you?"

"I didn't think I did. I'm so happy here, Will. I never imagined a place like this, with the magic sky, the light, the mountains. Just the—the freedom of it all. But I started to think about all the things we took for granted when we were young. That effortless feeling of knowing where we belonged, what we were supposed to do. Not that we always wanted to do it . . ."

Will laughed. "But we *knew*. I remember it well. I do wonder sometimes what I would be like if I'd stayed, gone into law like my brothers. Maybe I'd be less lonely. But that work would have killed me. I think being a society matron would have done the same for you."

"I think you're right." They reached the corner and

he twirled her around, making her giggle even as she felt almost overwhelmed by the wistful memories. "Are you really lonely, Will dear?"

"You don't need to look so sad, Maddie. I'm usually much too busy to think about my barren state."

"And not all alone, I would bet. You're such a handsome devil, Will Royle, as you've always well known. You must have lots of starlet girlfriends."

"None as sweet and gorgeous as you. And the starlets are all as busy as I am. The movie world is no career for sissies. You have to be hard-hearted."

"I have a difficult time thinking that of you. You've always been the perfect courteous gentleman—except that time you toppled me into the snow while we were sledding in Central Park and I ruined my new kid boots."

"That was an accident!"

"Hmm, was it? And when it comes to romance, what about Lorelei Fontaine, then?"

"I've never pushed her into the snow. It never snows in California."

"I mean—surely you two make time from your work for each other?"

"Once in a while. But I told you, really we're just friends. We understand each other, help each other."

"That's what she said, too." She glanced at Lorelei dancing with Rex Neville, though they were barely dancing now, their steps slow as they whispered fiercely to each other. Had it been like that with her and Luther Bishop, too, back in France or New Jersey? How baffling movie romances were! "If you're just friends . . ."

"Why, Mads! Are you asking me on a date?" Will gasped, his eyes going comically wide. "Whatever would your handsome doctor say?"

Maddie searched the crowd for a glimpse of David and found him dancing with Bridget Bishop. He was smiling at whatever she was saying, the shadows gone from his eyes for the moment. She wondered what he *would* say. What were they to each other, really? She sighed. "I wish I knew. You are so right, Will. Our old life had a certainty to it all. Now, anything can happen."

Will nodded. "It's scary, isn't it?"

"Scary, yes." Also intriguing. It made her head spin, like climbing up into the thin, clear air at the tip of the Sangre de Cristo mountains too fast. The whole, new world lay below those peaks. What part of it did she really want?

"What will you all do now about the movie?" she asked.

"Stay on, I guess. Bridget knows what she's doing. She has a calm decisiveness Luther was lacking. If she can take hold of the reins firmly enough, the studio will let it continue. I hope."

"Even with a police investigation? And the scandal? Will it be like William Desmond Taylor or something?"

Will frowned. "It's a concern, true. We all have to think of our careers, our reputations. Hopefully we're far enough away that all the details won't leak back until *The Far Sunset* is wrapped and everyone sees how good it is."

Maddie thought of Evie DuLaps and her notebooks. "I hope so."

"You know more about what goes on here than we do. What do you think will happen with the police?"

Maddie remembered Inspector Sadler. "I doubt they're too concerned about being discreet, to be honest. Inspector Sadler was brought in to clean things up, I think; he's always banging on about such things when I see him. But the department is very small, and most officers not as, shall we say, energetic as he is. If he finds out what happened quickly, I don't think he'll bother you much." *If he gets Gwen.* That's what she was worried about now.

Will snorted. "Good luck to him with that."

"Do *you* know anything about what happened?"

"Not a thing, Mads dearest, and that's the truth. I didn't have anything to do with it all. I stayed out of Luther's way whenever possible. But no one really liked him."

"So I've gathered."

"Will, darling, I absolutely *must* talk to you," Lorelei interrupted them. She danced up to them in Rex's arms, smiling but strained. "A small problem with one of the new scenes . . ."

"Of course," Will answered. He gave Maddie a rueful smile. "Work calls. See you later this evening?"

"Sure," she said. He danced off with Lorelei, leaving Maddie standing in the middle of the swirling dancers with Rex.

"Shall we, Mrs. Alwin?" he asked, and she nodded. He took her into his arms in place of Lorelei and led her smoothly back into the steps as if she had never stopped.

For a minute, she felt bowled over to actually be dancing with Rex Neville. Unlike so many actors, who seemed smaller, more human off the screen and out of makeup, he was even more gorgeous close up, his face as sculpted and sharp as the mountains, his eyes endless dark pools. He also smelled delicious and was a wonderful dancer. He gave her a smile as smooth as his dancing, the intense quiet of his interactions with Lorelei vanished. She couldn't wait to tell Juanita about it all.

"Is this the first project you've worked on with Lorelei Fontaine, then?" she finally managed to say, hoping her voice didn't come out too squeaky.

"Oh, no, we've been on lots of films together," he said. "She has an excellent eye for what clothes will project well. She makes us all look better."

Maddie wasn't sure he really needed any help with that. "But she wants to act instead?"

"Everyone wants to try acting. I've told her she should stay with her true talent."

Maddie wondered if that was what he and Lorelei had talked about as they danced. "And the Bishops? Have you worked with them before?"

"No. Luther always seemed like such a pill; I didn't want to be bothered. But he's so well known, my agent said everyone had to do one of his films sometime."

And yet she remembered Rex had meant to go to Germany to do an artsy film there. And there were those photos in Bishop's lockbox. "And that's how you ended up here?"

A flash of anger crossed his face, quickly covered by his smile. "I trusted my agent to get the best contract, one with a few loopholes. I shouldn't have."

"I guess we should all follow our instincts, especially when it comes to work. We have to be true to our own artistry."

"You are so right, Mrs. Alwin. Art always must come first. It's our reason for being."

Even beyond romance? Or, say, being murderous when things went wrong? Maddie wondered what Rex would do to get out of his contract and go to Germany. "What sort of roles would best express your artistry, do you think?"

"Something more complex than just being a matinee

idol. Something that delves into the mysteries of the human mind, all its complexities. Good and evil all mixed up."

"Really?" Maddie said. "That is fascinating. I often feel the same way. People are endlessly surprising."

"I told Lorelei she should try a different kind of film as well. Something more European. In Hollywood, everyone just wants to look good, to be fashionable. Fancy couture, whether it fits the character or not. In Europe, directors can use the style to fit the character. It all slots together in one seamless whole, a brand-new, real world." He twirled her under his arm. "A hack like Luther Bishop could never do that."

"Is it true that Bridget is taking over the production? Is she a hack, too?" Maddie said, a bit breathless from the spin.

"It's too early to say. She's certainly a fine actress, abominably treated by her husband. She's never directed before, but I'm sure she can't do worse." His voice lowered, almost as if he spoke to himself. "Maybe it will be worth it in the end."

Before Maddie could ask him what he meant by those strange words, the music came to an end and Rex left her by the fireplace. She noticed Gunther and Phil talking quietly at a nearby table, but Will and Lorelei had vanished.

"Madeline, my dear!" Bridget called as she handed David back to Maddie. "Do come and see me tomorrow. We have so much to talk about."

Maddie had only time to nod before Bridget swirled away again, in a cloud of chiffon and cigarette smoke. No Jicky perfume, though. Only Shalimar.

David handed her a Pink Lady cocktail disguised in a teacup. "Having fun?" he asked with a smile. "I didn't know you were such a grand dancer."

"Hmm. We've never danced together, have we? I learned all sorts of things from the teachers my mother insisted on in New York."

"Something to put right, definitely." He frowned a bit as he looked out at the crowd. "I'm sorry for earlier. I never should have spoiled the party with my own morbid thoughts. This Bishop business must be getting to me."

"Oh, no!" Maddie cried. "I want to know all your thoughts, David. I want to know—well, everything about you." And she realized it was true. She *did* want to know everything, and what was scarier, she wanted to tell him her secrets, too. Her past, her fears, her hopes. She hadn't wanted that with someone in so long.

He looked down at her, his eyes dark. "And I want that with you, too. Start with a dance?"

The song "June Moon" started on the gramophone. She finished her drink, and was distracted by a sudden, pale flash in the courtyard beyond the window. When she looked closer, she saw it was Evie DuLaps out there, in her unmistakable hat. She was talking to a man who looked somehow familiar, but they were in the shadows, and then vanished into the night.

Maddie shook her head. Maybe the Bishop business was "getting to her" as well.

CHAPTER 16

The next morning, Maddie headed to La Fonda to find Bridget Bishop. Maddie had already stopped to see Gwen at the jail, where her lawyer, Frank Springer, was there to consult with them, but maybe Bridget knew California attorneys or could find a way to help Gwen out even sooner. The more people on Gwen's side now, the better.

She found Bridget at a table in the corner of the lobby. Even though other guests, bellhops with luggage carts, and maids with their brooms and dust cloths swirled past her, she seemed absorbed in her own world. There were piles of papers stacked in front of her, letters and what looked like theater scripts, with Rex Neville's battered copy of Goethe on top. Bridget frowned as she looked them over, signing a few and setting one or two aside.

"Bridget," Maddie called as she rushed across the lobby,

dodging around chairs and tables, a lady with a poodle on a pearl lead.

"Oh, Maddie, I'm glad you're here, I wanted to ask you about the layout for this scene . . ." Bridget glanced up, and her eyes widened. "Jeepers, but you do look knackered. Sit down; tell me what's wrong. Waiter, could you bring us some tea?"

Maddie dropped into the chair across from Bridget. She *did* feel a bit "knackered," out of breath after her near-dash across town from the jail, but Bridget didn't press her. She just watched Maddie in careful, close concern and calmly poured out the tea when it arrived. Her cool presence was steadying, and Maddie could see how it served her well as a director.

Could such cool-headedness also have served her well in getting rid of her troublesome husband? Maddie wished she knew, that she had some kind of magical mirror that could see into people's thoughts. She told Bridget about the plans for Gwen's defense, and how Sadler was determined to solve the case quickly.

"It's all utterly ridic. I know Luther was an absolute swine to her, and that she's far too sweet to have grown the rhino hide a girl needs in Hollywood, but surely she wouldn't—no, I *know* she wouldn't. She couldn't. How on earth do they think a girl who weighs ninety pounds soaking wet could do that?" Bridget said.

"I don't know. I called Frank Springer, the attorney. He's the best lawyer in the state. He helped someone I know out of just such a sticky situation not long ago. He'll be able to find out more than I can. But in the meantime—is there anything at all you can tell me that might help her?"

Bridget tapped her pen on the papers, frowning in thought. "I can call my own lawyer in California, of course, so we can get more legal advice, but if you're asking if I have any idea what really happened to Luther— I'm afraid not. He wasn't the most popular person, of course, and I can't deny any number of us have easier lives now that my husband has gone. If we killed everyone who annoyed us, though, there would be no time for anything else! I tend to think it was the work of some passing maniac. We are so isolated out here."

"I wish it *was* a passing maniac, but it would have been a very well-organized one. A maniac prepared with morphine injections and ropes." Unless Harry Kelly could be considered a "passing maniac," if indeed the rejected actor really was in town.

Bridget gave a helpless shrug. "Well, I'm sure it wasn't poor little Gwen. Or myself, though I'd be happy to shake the hand of whoever it was. Other than that . . ."

"I know," Maddie sighed. "It really could be almost anyone."

"We actors are a tough lot, Madeline. We have to be, to get ahead. Though actors weren't the only ones who hated my husband. He owed money to nearly every bookie and bootlegger in California, and large portions of New York. Not to mention restaurants, tailors, jewelers. Irate fathers and husbands. I could go on."

Maddie nodded, thinking of Maria Ortiz and other girls like her. She studied Bridget carefully, wondering what she hid behind her beautiful actress's face. Maddie's instincts told her Bridget really hadn't done it, but then again, Bridget was a very good actress.

She picked up the volume of Goethe and turned it over. "Is Rex Neville trying to get you to film old German novels now?"

Bridget laughed. "In fact, he is. A great costume epic, with him as Young Werther, of course. It's not a terrible idea, if *The Far Sunset* does well. Which is looking less likely by the moment, if my cast keeps getting arrested."

"Is Rex no longer as angry about losing his German film, then?"

"We had a long talk this morning. I will shorten his part and move up the filming of his last scenes so he can go to Berlin, if he'll come back and do his next picture with me next year. Of course, without Gwen, how can I do his scenes now? They're love interests." Bridget sighed and shoved back a stack of papers. "He also gave me a bit of surprising news. He and Lorelei are engaged. I wonder if she could step into Gwen's part? There would be so much to reshoot, though."

So Eddie's hotel gossip had been right. "They're engaged?"

"I know, it's a bit weird, isn't it? I didn't even realize they knew each other that well. I thought she liked Will. But fans do love a wedding. It could be good publicity."

As Maddie thought over this bit of news, she idly flipped through the pages of the Goethe. Rex's name was written on the inside of the battered cover, and there were a few lines underlined on the pages. *Rex Neville*, it said, dark and blocky. She paused to study it. It looked like—like the writing on some of those notes to Luther, the ones Gwen swore she hadn't written. The note in her studio.

"Oh, actors," Bridget said, glancing at the book. "It's surprising how often they're semiliterate brutes. At least you can read Rex's writing, even though he prints like a schoolkid. Most of them have illegible scrawls."

"This is how Rex writes all the time?"

"Yes. Though I guess he's not too bad off in the brains department, if he loves Goethe so much. Oh, look, there's the happy bride now."

Maddie turned to see that Lorelei had just rushed into the lobby, but she didn't look especially *happy*. Her hair was straggling from its pins, her cheeks frantically pink as her gaze darted around the crowd. She ran toward Bridget, her satin backless mules clacking on the tile floor.

"I've been burgled!" Lorelei gasped, skidding to a stop beside their table.

"Burgled?" Bridget said. "What do you mean? What's gone?"

"Some of my jewelry. It's not on my dressing table now!"

Bridget frowned. "Are you sure that's where you left it? I am sorry, Lorelei, but you're not the tidiest. Could it just be somewhere else?"

"Of course not! First murders, now thefts." Lorelei's voice rose to almost a shriek, making people nearby look at her in shock. "I want to talk to that manager!"

Maddie was surprised that Lorelei, a woman who had nursed in France and worked her way up in the labyrinth of the film world, was behaving like that. It was true that the events of the past few days had been terrible, but why such a sudden descent? She stood up and took Lorelei's arm. She was trembling.

"I'm sure Anton would be quite happy to help," Maddie said softly. "Maybe I could help you take another look first? I'm always finding lost things in the strangest places. I put a diamond earring in my watercolor box once; I have no idea why!"

For a second, she was afraid Lorelei would protest, pull away. Her mouth opened, but then she seemed to melt, and nodded. Maddie led her away, toward her room. She glanced back at Bridget, who mouthed a *thank you*.

Lorelei's room was indeed just as messy as it had been when Maddie last saw it, maybe even worse. Dresses and shawls were scattered over every piece of furniture, shoes littered the floor, and there were layers of scarves, cosmetics, and perfume bottles on the dressing table. She saw the red shawl Lorelei had worn at the dance. Had it been only last night? It felt like years. Maddie couldn't believe the woman she'd chatted with over champagne that night was the same teary, unsteady Lorelei who stood hesitantly just inside the door.

"Now, let's have a little look," Maddie said briskly. She folded up a tumble of silk slips and camisoles and tucked them into a drawer. There were papers there, torn envelopes, something that looked like pages from a book. "Where could they be? Where do you usually change clothes? Maybe the jewelry got caught in a garment."

"Behind that dressing screen. You really are a darling to help, Maddie."

Maddie glanced at the painted screen in the corner. A white dressing gown was tossed over it, a stain on the sleeve. "Of course. I know the last few days have been a strain. What exactly is it that's lost?"

Lorelei ran a shaking hand over her cheek. "Oh, a clip. A gold one, I wore it in my hair. It's quite special to me. And maybe a pair of aquamarine earrings?" She knelt down to peer under the bed as Maddie sorted through the jumble on the table.

"Bridget tells me you're engaged," Maddie said, putting away a string of red beads. "Congratulations! You'll be the envy of half the women in America."

Lorelei laughed shakily. "Oh. Yes. I'll have to get to work designing a gown."

"Will you get married before or after he goes to Germany?"

"We haven't really talked about it." Lorelei's voice was muffled by the bed. "It's all so sudden."

"A whirlwind romance?"

"Something like that. He's—well, you've seen him. How could I resist?"

"I know what you mean." Maddie capped a rouge pot and tucked a few half-used lipsticks into a vanity case. There was no gold clip. She wondered if Lorelei might hire a maid after she was married.

One of the lipsticks was a familiar filigreed tube. Maddie rolled it up, already knowing what she would see— Ravishing Rose, the tip worn away. Was it some kind of clue? But then again, every woman in Santa Fe seemed to wear the stuff. And Luther had had a *lot* of girlfriends, the cad. She thought Lorelei had worn dark red at the dance. Maybe the lipstick wasn't even hers at all.

She tucked it away and turned to the small writing

desk, which was covered with sketches of dresses and hats. There was an empty glass there and a full ashtray, and she took them to the little powder room to rinse out. She took a quick whiff—whiskey. Maybe that would explain Lorelei's shaky behavior. Or maybe Rex had given her something stronger, if he regularly behaved like he had in those photos.

A jolt of cold fear shivered through her as she wondered if Lorelei was next.

She put away the glass and ashtray in a cupboard and picked up a pile of used towels scattered on the brightly colored tiles of the floor. They didn't smell of Shalimar, but of something sharper, smokier, like a man's expensive cologne. But that would make sense if she was engaged to Rex. Of course he would be in her room.

As Maddie shook one of the towels, something tumbled out and landed with a metallic click near the bathtub. She scooped it up and saw it was a gold, leaf-shaped clip, like the one Gwen owned, the ones in Luther Bishop's jeweler's receipt. It was broken, the sharp clip part on the back snapped in two. A bit of something black and sticky was caught there. Melted bakelite or something?

She took it back to the bedroom, where Lorelei was sorting through one of her trunks. "Is this it?"

"Oh, yes!" Lorelei's expression brightened as she reached for it. "Wherever did you find it? I was afraid it was gone for good, and it was—well, a special present."

"Caught in one of the bathroom towels."

"How silly! I must have kept it in my hair when I was washing it." She turned it over and frowned. "But it's broken. Snapped right through."

"Maybe that's why it fell out?" Maddie said. Lorelei didn't answer, just stared down at the clip as if mesmerized. Maddie was quite worried about her. "Here, Lorelei, why don't you take a little nap? I'll have some food sent in, too. A rest would do you good."

"Yes," Lorelei murmured. "I think I will." She let Maddie tuck her into bed and turn the lights out. When Maddie made her way to the door, her eyes were already closed.

Maddie found a maid and asked her to have a tray sent to Lorelei's room, and made her way back toward the lobby to tell Bridget what had happened. At the end of the corridor, she ran into Rex Neville.

He was just as handsome as ever, with those deep, dreamy eyes, the cut-glass angles of his face that the camera loved so much, a charming flash of a smile. But after having seen how Lorelei was reacting to being engaged to him, Maddie was no longer quite so sure about the man.

"I hear congratulations are in order," she said.

"Oh, yes!" he answered, his whole face lighting up with joy. "I'm going to Germany after all. Just got a telegram from the director. They're going to hold the part for me for a few weeks."

"That's lovely. But I really meant your engagement. To Lorelei."

"Oh. Yeah. That's great, too, sure. Everything seems to be looking up for me finally."

"I'm glad." Maddie glanced back over her shoulder at Lorelei's closed door. "I just left your fiancée. She wasn't in very good shape, I'm afraid. I had a maid send in some food. She looked like she hasn't eaten in a while."

"I'll just go check on her, then. Good to see you, Mrs. Alwin."

"You, too." Maddie watched him saunter toward Lorelei's room, his hands in his pockets, whistling. Odd for a man whose fiancée was ill. But then again, Maddie was no longer surprised by any odd things these people did. Was she getting used to them, then? Scary thought.

She made her way to the lobby, tugging on her gloves as she thought of all the strange happenings in the last few days. Would everything go back to normal once Bridget Bishop and her movie left town? Would her quiet days working and evenings having a drink with friends come back again? Or was it all changed for good?

She turned a corner and nearly ran into Bill Ackerman, the cameraman. He had one of his hand-rolled cigarettes clenched between his lips but unlit, and he looked as distracted and anxious as she felt herself.

"Oh, hello, Mr. Ackerman!" she said. "How is your camera? Were you able to fix it?"

"Hey, Mrs. Alwin," he said with a smile. "Nice to see you. No, not yet. Damned thing was cut straight through. Infuriating. I had to order a new sprocket. It's coming out from California by express, but we're at a bit of standstill now. I'm meeting with Bridget to talk about what to do in the meantime. I don't suppose you know anything about film?"

"If it's not a paintbrush, I'm afraid I can't help you," she answered ruefully. "But I did see Bridget in the lobby earlier. Let me walk back there with you."

They strolled through the crowds hurrying toward their rooms, Maddie asking him more questions about the workings of cameras and if he had such problems often. In the lobby, Bridget stood next to her desk, laughing flirtatiously up at the man who stood beside her. He was quite tall, probably the tallest man Maddie had seen in the movies, with a thick tumble of dark, curly hair and a weathered face that was still quite ruggedly handsome. Handsome—and familiar.

"Maddie, Bill!" Bridget called merrily. "Do come say hello to our new leading man, who so gallantly answered my emergency summons from Hollywood. We will kill Rex off halfway through the film, and a new hero will appear. This is Harry Kelly."

CHAPTER 17

Maddie's house smelled delicious when she stepped inside, of green chili stew and fresh bread baking, and it was all so warm and welcoming. Exactly what she needed after her long, strange day. She took off her hat and gloves and hurried into the kitchen.

Juanita sat at the table with Father Malone, the two of them going over what looked like a rota for the altar flowers at the cathedral. Father Malone looked so friendly, so cheerful in his glinting eyeglasses, with his thinning pale hair, his kind eyes, she couldn't help but be glad to see him again.

"Father Malone, how lovely that you're here," she said, leaning over to take a long, lovely sniff of the simmering stew.

"And you, Mrs. Alwin. I brought back the copy of *The Secret of Dunstan's Tower* you sent to me; it was delightful. I couldn't put it down."

Maddie sat across from them at the table and reached for the coffee pot. Juanita jumped up to fetch a plate of her marvelous biscochitos, and Maddie bit into one with a grateful sigh. She hadn't realized how hungry she was. Snooping about took a lot of energy. "I'm so glad you liked it."

"I don't suppose you have any others you've read recently I could borrow? Oh, no, I imagine you haven't had the time. The troubles that have been happening and everything."

Maddie sighed again, this time with weariness. "Yes, and more trouble all the time. I suppose you remember my poor cousin was hauled off to jail by Inspector Sadler?"

"Yes, of course. But you don't think Miss Astor did it?"

"No, I don't. It's true she hasn't really been herself, or at least not the Gwen I used to know, but I can't imagine she's capable of murder. Not to mention it would be physically impossible for her to do it alone."

"And there are so many other people who could have done it," Juanita said. "Mr. Bishop was not a good man, Father."

"No, he wasn't. We even made a list of suspects." Maddie found her sketchbook in the pile of movie mags and showed him the suspects she and Juanita had considered. "I doubt we even know half the *real* suspects, though."

"Interesting," Father Malone murmured as he peered at the scribbled list through his gleaming spectacles.

"I was just at La Fonda, Juanita, and you won't believe it. Harry Kelly is here to take over leading-man duties!" Maddie said. "And Lorelei Fontaine and Rex Neville are engaged!"

"Are they?" Juanita gasped. "They don't seem very close at all."

"I know. And Lorelei doesn't seem the glowing bride-to-be today. In fact, she seemed a bit ill." Maddie bit her lip as she remembered Lorelei, looking so frail tucked into her bed, her hysteria over a jewel that wasn't even really lost, just broken. "In fact, she reminded me of how Gwen was when she first arrived here, exhausted and fragile."

Father Malone gave her a sympathetic glance. "Drugs, maybe? I've heard movie people are notorious for them, with all the help they need to keep such long hours."

"I don't know, though it's a possibility. Luther Bishop had morphine in his system, though it looks like the killer gave it to him rather than it being self-inflicted. I saw Bridget Bishop today, too, and met Harry Kelly; neither of them looked like they were oofy on something. You know of Harry Kelly, the actor, right, Juanita? From the magazines. Bridget says she's hiring him, though I think I saw him earlier, with Evelyn at the dance."

"Maybe Miss DuLaps had the scoop he was joining the cast?" Juanita said.

"Possibly. Oh, I wish I could see Evelyn's notebook! It

must be a doozy." Maddie tapped her fingernail on the list. "Do you have any ideas, Father Malone?"

"Too many, I'm afraid," he sighed. "Remember what Father Brown said in *The White Pillars Murder*? Detectives don't catch criminals by 'smelling their hair-oil or counting their buttons.' They do it by 'being half-criminals themselves.' This is a strange case. We just need to think how this murderer would have thought, what his reasoning must have been."

Maddie laughed. "Must we go on a crime spree, then? I bet your archbishop wouldn't like that!"

"I wish we could; it might be fun," Father Malone said, rather wistfully, and Maddie wondered what he had really gotten up to in his misspent Boston youth, before he found the priesthood and went off to the Western missions. "But it's a bit like being a priest, isn't it? Or an artist. Hearing people's confessions, understanding what's in their hearts, what makes them act as they do. We must learn to think as others might."

"And what their real motivations might have been in getting rid of Luther Bishop?"

"Of course. The first and most obvious motive is always love turned to hate. It sounds as if Mr. Bishop had many amours. Perhaps his wife had enough, or one of his girlfriends begged him to take her back and he refused. Maybe he had promised her marriage, or something else he couldn't deliver."

"I think Bridget's motive would have been he was holding back her career," Maddie said.

"Yes, ambition can also be very powerful. The fury of feeling thwarted, powerless. Fear, blackmail. Of course, most people, even when angry or feeling wronged, couldn't take a life. But there are those blinded by self. Who think what *they* want and desire is all that is important. Those people are very dangerous, because they don't see others as human."

"Yes," Maddie said. That could describe many of the movie crowd, their ambition and need for better parts, bigger films, overwhelming their better natures. It seemed Luther Bishop had stood in just about everyone's way, once they were of no use to him any longer. "David thinks it would have been hard for a woman to string the body up herself. But maybe one could have some help?"

"Of course. Who would have been the partner in crime, then?" Juanita said.

"Any of these men on your list, I suppose. So we are back where we started." Father Malone gave his head a rueful shake. "I wouldn't do Father Brown proud, I'm afraid."

After he left to get ready for afternoon Mass, Maddie took Buttercup out to the garden, watching in the mellow-amber light of late afternoon to make sure the dog didn't dig up any flower beds. She thought about Father Malone's list of motives—love, ambition, fury, blackmail—and how they applied to just about everyone on the movie set.

Who had loved the most? Who hated? Who was the most coldly ambitious, the most self-centered? Who was capable of cold-bloodedly killing, in order to get and protect what they thought was rightfully theirs? And who might crack up under the pressure?

Maddie paced along her garden paths, seeing not the red, yellow, and white tumble of flowers, the old salt cedar tree the twins used for a castle tower, the gleaming windows of her art studio. She saw the movie set. On the morning Luther was found dead, it had all been business as usual on the set, bustling and busy.

She closed her eyes and remembered the ghostly white flash atop the mesa that day on the set. Could it have been one of the flannel dressing gowns all the ladies wore over their costumes? Why would one of them have been on the mesa? It could have been anyone—Bridget, Lorelei, Gwen.

Lipstick, perfume, threatening notes, books. Ambition. Greed. Ego.

Of course. "How stupid I've been!" Maddie cried aloud, startling Buttercup into a bark. She ran into the house and snatched up the phone, dialing La Fonda. Bridget had gone to the movie set, and Lorelei's room wasn't answering. The front-desk receptionist thought Miss Fontaine

had left with Mr. Neville, but wasn't sure. A jolt of raw
fear went through Maddie at that bit of news.

"Juanita, I'll be back soon!" she called, catching up her
hat. "Call Inspector Sadler and tell him to go to the movie
set at once. It's an emergency." She ran into her room and
took Pete's old service revolver from her drawer, tucking
it and a box of ammunition into her handbag.

When she came back, Juanita was in the kitchen doorway, a dishcloth in her hand and a frown on her face.
"Señora Maddie, what on earth . . ."

"I have to go now! I'll tell all later, I promise. Call the
inspector?" She kept running, and dashed next door to
find Gunther and his typewriter on his portal. "Gunther,
darling, I *must* borrow the Duesy again, and you can't say
no. It's an absolute emergency."

Gunther immediately stood up and reached for his
jacket. "Oh, no, dearest. If you are running off on some
Boy's Own Adventure, I insist on going with you."

CHAPTER 18

The gates to the set were closed when Gunther pulled up in the Duesenberg, but not guarded. The sun was starting to set, the sky streaked with pink, gold, coral, lavender, and everything seemed quiet. Eerily quiet, considering the noise and commotion that usually swirled around there.

As Gunther jumped out to open the gate, Maddie studied the road ahead of them. Her stomach fluttered nervously, and the gun in her bag felt as heavy as a lead weight. She couldn't see anything, not even a cloud of dust to indicate someone was there.

Gunther climbed back into the car and sped past the gate. "Where to now?" he asked. Maddie had brought him up-to-date on her suspicions as they drove out of town. He had asked a few questions but never questioned her sanity, as she had done a bit herself. That was what she loved about Gunther—he was always a good ally.

"I'm not sure," she answered. "Where do you think they would go? Do you see anything?"

He had switched off the headlights to keep from giving away their arrival, and twilight was sweeping on fast now, swaths of deep midnight blue taking over the sky. He drew the Duesy to a stop behind a grove of cottonwoods near the river. Hardly daring to breathe, Maddie studied the deserted set. The wagon, the adobe walls, the cliffs stained blood red by the setting sun—it looked like a ghost town with no actors and camera crew around.

She turned to the main bungalow, where the makeup department, the wardrobe, and the offices were so busy during the day. Two cars were parked off to the side, and she glimpsed a flicker of light at one of the back windows. The only sign of life.

"They must be in there," she whispered. "Do you think there's another way in besides the front door?"

She had the thought that it might be more prudent to wait for Sadler, but then she realized there was no time to creep around cautiously waiting for a man who might or might not show up. A shrill scream pierced the night silence, so loud it echoed past the walls and windows.

Maddie pulled her gun from her handbag, quickly loaded it, and jumped out of the car to run toward the building. Somehow all her fear had vanished, burned up in a rush of raw excitement. A cold, clear steadiness made everything seem extra sharp in her mind, and she wondered if that was how her husband had felt in battle.

The long, narrow makeup room was dark, the mirrors glinting like a dozen eyes watching her, and for a second she worried they had come to the wrong place. But there was a ray of light at the end of the room, from the hallway that led to Luther Bishop's office, and another scream rang out. Someone shouted, a man's voice, high and sharp, as if fearful.

Maddie slipped off her shoes to keep her from making any noise that might startle them, and crept forward with her gun held level. Gunther followed her example, taking off his shoes and slipping silently down the hall with her. Maddie glanced down at the cold steel of the firearm in her hand. She had only done a bit of target practice in her garden a few times, but luckily it was steady in her grip, and she hoped it would at least make any villain think twice.

Gunther crept into the room with her, silent as a cat, and she was glad he had her back. Together they tiptoed around the hallway, the voices growing louder as they found the half-open door of the office.

The sight that greeted them was like a scene from a movie itself.

Bridget was tied to a chair, her eyes wide and terrified above a gag, the strongbox broken open and spilled at her feet. Letters and photographs were tangled on the carpet, some of them half burned. Rex Neville stood behind the desk, his hands in the air, his handsome face etched with a beseeching, defiant, fearful expression, all at once.

Lorelei was across the room—and she held a gun of her own trained on her fiancé. Unlike Maddie, her hands were not steady. The firearm wavered wildly in her grasp. Her hair spilled out of its combs, and her mascara streaked her pale cheeks. She didn't seem at all like the stylish, strong woman she'd once appeared, with a black coat tossed over a rumpled cotton frock and her stockings snagged. Shocked, Maddie peered closer and saw a possible explanation in Lorelei's dilated eyes. Was she on drugs, like those given to Luther before he was killed?

"You lied to me," Lorelei sobbed. "You never meant to do what you said at all!"

"You crazy broad," Rex said roughly. "I was going to marry you, wasn't I? What more did you want?"

"I wanted what you promised me! The part in this movie, and it was finally mine. All you had to do was finish the picture with me, and *then* go to Germany. But you sabotaged Bill Ackerman's camera, cut the film with my own hair clip. I would never get my chance!"

"The movie in Germany won't wait long. I had no choice! As Mrs. Rex Neville, you would have had plenty of other chances."

"I wanted *this* chance!" Lorelei shrieked. "You said if

I helped you with that one thing, if I found you the morphine, you would get me that chance. I even got Will to buy me those drugs. But you lied again and again. I thought it was just to make Luther more mellow, to make our jobs easier, but you—you killed him. I saw you string him up!"

So that was what had happened. Maddie hadn't been sure which of them had hatched the plan to hang Luther, probably hoping it would look like suicide, but it was Rex. Lorelei had gotten the drugs, and Rex had hanged the director. And Will—her old friend Will—had given Lorelei the morphine! She and Gunther exchanged startled glances.

"Hey, you know it wasn't like that," Rex said with a smile, obviously trying to recapture some of his famous charm even as his smile wobbled. "Luther stood in our way, in everyone's way. This picture was a disaster. You wanted a part in this movie, and I wanted to go to Germany, to show everyone I could be a real actor. He had to go. We agreed on it."

Lorelei gave her head a frantic shake. "No, not like that! I won't do this anymore!"

"You don't have a choice!" Rex shouted. He suddenly lashed out, hitting Lorelei hard in the face. She fell back, the gun falling from her hand and skittering across the floor, under the desk. Lorelei was still, too still, and Maddie knew she had to do something. She jumped out of their hiding place before Gunther could stop her and leveled her own weapon on Rex.

"What are you doing here?" he growled, and she wondered how she had ever thought him so handsome. He looked like a demon now, all glowing, furious eyes. He lunged toward her, but Maddie fired off a shot at the rafters, deafeningly loud in the small space, and he went very still. She could hear Bridget's sobs, Lorelei's ragged breath, Gunther slipping out behind her, and the unsteady pounding of her own heart, but time seemed frozen.

"I came to find out the truth," Maddie said. "I had worked most of it out, but now I see it all. You used poor Lorelei's own ambitions to get her to be your accomplice, you told her Luther would only be drugged, frightened, and then you made a noose and strung him up in his own office. And you let Gwen take the fall."

Rex grinned and shook the fall of his untidy dark hair back from his brow. But he didn't move. They faced each other like two wary predators in the primeval forest. "You're pretty ballsy for some society dame, aren't you? Someone had to take the blame. I can't worry about that. Right when I'm so close to having what I deserve. What's one little starlet, just like thousands of others, next to what I could be? Now, without Luther's interference, my career can really go places. Now, be good and give me that gun; you have no idea what to do with it. Once Bridget and Lorelei are gone, I'll have it all. Your

Gwen can swing just like Bishop, for all I care. For all anyone cares."

"No!" Maddie whispered, feeling cold with fear at facing down such pure evil. Her finger tightened on the trigger, and Gunther lunged forward to try to grab her before she could fire. He was a split second too late, and the shot exploded with a deafening roar in the small room. Bridget shrieked behind her gag. But the bullet landed in the floor next to Rex's foot, just like Maddie intended. She didn't want to miss seeing this guy where he belonged—in prison.

"You crazy bitch!" Rex shouted. He made a dive for Lorelei's lost gun.

"Oh, no, you don't!" Maddie yelled. She dashed toward him, aiming her own gun at Rex again, but Bridget managed to trip him by shooting out her unbound leg, and Gunther tackled him. Maddie struggled to aim at Rex and not the others.

There was a sudden roar of engines outside the window, a glare of headlights. Maddie heard the door to the bungalow burst open, the clatter of running, booted feet. "Everyone freeze! Now!" Sadler bellowed, and she had never been so happy to see that annoying man in her life.

Rex punched Bridget in the face, making her chair fall back, and he leaped to his feet to make a run for it. He shoved a policeman out of his way and was halfway out the door.

Maddie raised her gun, feeling that cool, icy sensation come over her again, and she fired off a shot at the wall, to the left of Rex. Fragments of thin plaster flew in a shower of powdery white, and Rex, startled, tripped to the floor just in time to be grabbed by Inspector Sadler's meaty fist. His shouts were thunderous as he was hauled away, protestations of his innocence and Lorelei's guilt ignored.

Lorelei still huddled on the floor, but Maddie could see that her eyes were open and she was breathing. Gunther hurried to untie Bridget, and Maddie helped Lorelei to sit up.

"He was going to kill me," Bridget cried. "All for the sake of getting out of the film, the rotten bastard! And you, Lorelei, you ungrateful whore, you helped him. You're fired."

"Are you both all right?' Maddie asked, hunting in the desk drawers for some medicinal hooch. Bridget surely could use a little nip just then—they all could.

"Just a little knock on the head, but my Irish skull is too thick for his pitiful taps," Bridget said, rubbing at her wrists. "He said he had to talk to me urgently about his part, and when I turned away for a second—bam. I should have known better than to turn my back on him, the snake. Actors who are too good-looking are always rotten." She gave Lorelei a glance, half pitying, half scornful. "Now what on earth are we going to do with *her*?"

CHAPTER 19

"So it was Rex and Lorelei all along?" Gwen gasped. She took a big bite of Juanita's special, rarely baked cure-all chocolate-cherry cake, and shook her head. She didn't look too much the worse for her jail ordeal. In fact, she looked better than Maddie had seen her since she'd arrived in Santa Fe, more like her old laughing self again. She ate her cake and followed the story as avidly as if it had been one of their favorite romance novels when they were girls in New York.

As the dawn light outside turned the burnished wood floors of Maddie's house into rosy pink, her kitchen was packed, with Gwen, Gunther, Bridget, Francisco, Eddie and the girls, Father Malone, and David all crowded around the table to feast on cake and coffee as they went over the shocking, sordid tale. Maddie wouldn't have been surprised if it all became a Bridget Bishop Production one day—murder, blackmail, drugs, and scandal all up on the silver screen.

"So it seems," Maddie said, "Inspector Sadler has Rex at the jail now, and I'm sure he'll have the whole story out of him soon. It seems he thought if Luther was gone, the film would stop and he would be released so he could go to Germany."

"What about Lorelei, then?" Gwen asked.

"She was taken to St. Vincent's, almost catatonic at first," David said. "Once she had some fluids and a sedative, she wanted to talk. She says Rex Neville promised to get her the acting job she wanted; they just had to render Luther Bishop more—amenable."

"With morphine," Bridget said.

"Yes," David answered. "Miss Fontaine says she thought they were only going to drug him. But Rex gave him too much and killed him instead, on purpose, and strung him up hoping it would look like a suicide. He told her that if she went to the police, she would surely be implicated in the murder. And worse, according to her, once she got the part she wanted, he set about sabotaging the movie before she had even filmed her first scene so he could take off for Germany."

"Just like in *The Head of Caesar*," Father Malone said.

"Luther was always scolding Rex about his drug use," Bridget said. "It couldn't have made his thinking any clearer. I'm sure the inspector will get all the answers out of that swine anyway. I've seen people be fools for love and money before, of course, and extreme ambition isn't exactly rare in our business. But who would have thought people would *kill* for it? I don't understand what Rex was thinking at all. He was about to get all he could have wanted."

"Surely some people have no sense of an ordinary human conscience," David said. "A doctor friend of mine in London has started applying Jungian psychology to some of his patients and tells me he's encountered just such people. They feel they are the only ones who matter; everyone else is merely a pawn to get what they desire. I wonder what he would make of Mr. Neville?"

"It sounds like my husband, as well," said Bridget. "What delicious irony that his own faults were his downfall!"

"A lesson for us all," Father Malone said.

Maddie poured out another cup of coffee, trying to keep from yawning after the long night. "What about the movie, then?"

Bridget took a bite of cake. "It depends on what we hear of the financing, of course. This is all bound to be such an enormous scandal!"

"But think of the publicity," Francisco said.

"True. Everyone will be fainting with curiosity!"

Bridget answered with delight. "I want to continue film-ing. Harry Kelly can take on the part of love interest, once we do a little dicing and splicing and kill Rex off in the story, and if we work fast we can be done in only a few weeks now. Maybe not even that long. If Mrs. Anaya can take over wardrobe duties?"

Juanita glanced at Francisco and blushed. She had already told Maddie that once the movie was over, Fran-cisco planned to go back to visit his family at the pueblo instead of returning to California at once. Maddie hoped that meant the newly reunited couple could spend more time together again. "That would be interesting."

But the other blossoming couple, Phil Ballard and Gunther, sat far apart from each other, not looking at each other, not talking. Phil had already said he had two more roles lined up for the year and would be leav-ing soon. Maybe Gunther was right—never the twain shall meet—yet she still ached for him. Surely there was something, someone, out there who would make her friend happy?

Maddie glanced at Gwen, who was staring down at her half-eaten cake with a distracted frown. Gwen put down her fork and slipped out the door into the garden while everyone talked about the adjustments to be made to filming. Worried, Maddie followed her.

The dawn light was brighter now, a golden glow over the flowers, turning the tan adobe walls of Maddie's house to pure pink. Gwen sat on the twins' swing tied to the old salt cedar, pushing herself back and forth as she studied the sunrise.

"Are you feeling all right, Gwennie?" Maddie asked. "I'm sure David could give you something to help you sleep."

Gwen gave her a crooked little smile. She looked older now, even older than she had when she'd first arrived in Santa Fe, sad and serious. "I'm fine, Maddie, really. Not tired at all. Just a little—numb, I guess."

Maddie sat down on a patch of grass and stretched her legs out into the first reaching rays of sun. She let the peace of the morning, the trees and the flowers, wash over her. It felt like a new day indeed. "So much has happened in such a short time. It's very head-spinning. No wonder you feel numb. I can't process it at all."

"Exactly. It was like I was asleep, caught in a dream, and now I've finally woken up." Gwen pushed at the grass with her bare toe, setting the swing to swaying. "I've been such a fool. Getting involved with Luther, letting my vanity take over. I'm lucky it stopped before I became crazy like Rex!"

"That would never have happened, Gwen. We all lose ourselves sometimes. The world can make us all a little crazy, can't it? But your kind heart will always be there. That can't change."

"Can't it? I do wonder. I could so easily have been

Lorelei, letting things get so distorted I no longer knew what was up or down." She leaned back and stared up into the tree limbs, as if she could see some phantom past written there.

"What do you want to do now?"

"Finish the movie, I guess. I owe Bridget that. And then . . ."

"Then?"

"I think I might go back to New York. Take some proper acting lessons, maybe try my hand on the real stage. I've been missing home lately."

"Yes." Maddie studied the way the pure, clear light dappled her garden golden. She'd also been thinking about the idea of *home*. Seeing Gwen and Will again had brought New York, old memories, closer than they had been in a long time. She'd been drawn to that past, to the certainties of the world she had known when she was a girl, but she also knew those times were completely gone. The girl she had been then was gone, burned away in loss and independence and seeing a new world. A world where she was as free of limits as the endless turquoise sky above her. New Mexico was her real home now, and Juanita and Eddie and the girls her family.

"Lady Macbeth, then?" Maddie asked, feeling suddenly light as air.

Gwen smiled. "Maybe. Eventually."

Will came out the kitchen door, grinning as he saw

them there. "There you two are! Sharing secrets out here?"

"I've decided to go back to New York," Gwen said. "Become the new Ellen Terry."

"You'll be great," he said, pushing Gwen's swing so high she squealed.

"And what will you do, Will?" Maddie asked. She sincerely hoped he wouldn't supply anyone else with morphine ever again.

"I don't know. Work on new film scenes, I guess. I can't go back to New York. The weather's too cold for me now that I'm a California boy."

"Maybe be more careful about picking your girl-friends in the future?" Gwen said.

"Hey, Lorelei wasn't always such a mess! It's really sad," Will protested. "But you're right. I've had it with actresses. She told me she needed morphine for a toothache, and like a chump I got it for her, at the risk of my own reputation. I'm on the lookout for something real again." He gave Maddie a sad glance, a quirky smile she knew was good-bye. "I don't suppose *you* could be tempted to come to California, Maddie? Keep on working in art direction?"

"Or come back to New York with me?" said Gwen. "We don't have to go back to our horrid families. We could share a cold-water flat in the Village, and have fun horrifying our mothers with our flapperish behavior!"

Maddie studied her garden, her little house. She

caught a glimpse of Juanita and Francisco in the kitchen window, washing dishes together, and Buttercup came bounding outside, barking. It made her feel wonderfully at peace. This was hers, something her very own. "I think I'll stay right here."

Gwen and Will soon wandered back into the house, and after a few minutes of watching the sun inching up into the sky, Maddie stood to follow them. She leaned against the tree, letting its old strength, the strength of the land around her, hold her up.

"There you are," she heard David say. She turned to see him coming down the path from the kitchen door, his hair sparkling silvery in the early light, his eyes crinkled at the edges with his smile. It made her feel warm all over to see him there, something she had once thought she would never know again after Pete died. But she was coming to life all over again with the morning. "Are you feeling well, Maddie? It's been a strange night."

"Oh, yes. Better than I have in ages, in fact." She smiled and held out her hand to him. He took it between both of his, warm and steady and strong. "I was just thinking about home."

He leaned against the tree next to her, their fingers entwined. "Home?"

"Yes. Life does like to throw all sorts of unexpected challenges at us, doesn't it?" She thought of her old life in New York, of Pete and what her hopes had once been.

Of David's poor wife, of all he had seen in the war. And somehow they had ended up there, in a Santa Fe garden, together. "War, illness, even murder. But sometimes it gives us a rare gift, too. A place where we can belong. People who understand us. Families we never expect."

"That's true. The world is terrible—and also glorious."

"Then we should appreciate those gifts, shouldn't we? Hold on to them as tightly as we can?"

He smiled down at her, his eyes as blue as the sky. "I think that you, Madeline Alwin, are a very wise woman." He leaned down to kiss her, and she fancied she felt all the world in that one kiss.

She held on to him there in the Santa Fe sunshine, and all felt like it had suddenly fallen into a wonderful place. The very place she had always been meant to be.

AUTHOR'S NOTE

I've always loved silent movies! There's just something about the deep emotion of the actors' expressive faces, the intimacy of being in that world with them, that can't be found anywhere else. The stars just seemed grander— Mary Pickford, Douglas Fairbanks, Charlie Chaplin, Lillian Gish—as do the surroundings. A silent movie set, surrounded by big personalities and great artists with often clashing visions and egos, seemed like the perfect place for murder . . .

And the early 1920s was the perfect time. Film was still young, still experimental in many ways, but not in its infancy. It was becoming more sophisticated all the time (Griffith's *Intolerance* came out in 1916; United Artists was formed in 1919 and reformed how films were distributed). Movies were getting bigger, more complex, more artistic; more women were in top spots, not just as actresses but as directors, writers, and artists, than at any other time. There were also many great scandals, à la the Bishops, which led to the formation of the Hays Code.

The Western was an interesting genre at the time. The West as an actual place, a reality of ranches and cowboys, overlapped the beginnings of film. It wasn't a distant, imagined past; some actors such as William S. Hart had actually grown up working as cowboys and insisted on reality in their films. Hollywood was even able to catch its last echoes on film (like the last great overland cattle drive). Location filming was becoming ever more popular, as audiences wanted an authentic appearance. I based *The Far Sunset* in part on *The Covered Wagon* (1923), an epic about a wagon train's tragic trek west, with a love triangle, one of the first films done on location. It was highly successful at the box office, but as far as I know, there were no murders in the making!

The school Pearl and Ruby attend, the Loretto Academy (or the Academy of Our Lady of Light) was first opened in 1853 by the Sisters of Loretto under the direction of Archbishop Lamy (of *Death Comes for the Archbishop* fame), with 300 students. There was a great demand for their services, and the school quickly expanded to a large campus. It included a beautiful chapel, modeled on the Sainte-Chapelle in Paris, complete with its Miraculous Staircase. (The chapel can still be visited and is a must-see on any trip to Santa Fe, but the school itself was closed in 1968 and sold off, after educating thousands of young ladies like the Anaya twins.)

Some sources I used in the research for *A Moment in Crime*:

—Mary J. Straw Cook, *Loretto: The Sisters and Their Santa Fe Chapel* (2002)

—*Silent Movie: The Birth of Film and the Triumph of Movie Culture*

—Louise Brooks, *Lulu in Hollywood* (2000)

—William K. Everson, *American Silent Film* (1998)

—Karen Brownlow, *The Parade Gone By* (1968)

—George Pratt, *Spellbound in Darkness* (1966)

—Jeanine Basinger, *Silent Stars* (1999)